Letters in t

Kit Rose

Letters in the Dark

A Dark Captive Romance

Prologue

The watcher smiled as he wiped the knife clean. Shimmering steel in a once sterile kitchen. Crimson and thick, the blood had pooled on the table under the man and was now running down his arm into a puddle on the tile dining room floor.

This was his gift to her. A gift of vengeance. A gift of blood and pain. The only gifts that mattered.

The man on her dining room table had wronged her. He'd lied to her, and he'd broken her trust. The watcher had known from the beginning, and he'd helped the woman find out. What else could he have done?

It hadn't worked. She'd been too kind once again. Somehow, after all these years, after all her torment, she was still so kind, so willing to forgive. Maybe that was how she had survived the monsters of her past.

She'd watched all the good things in her life burn, and in the ashes, she'd found only heartache. She should have been broken like him. Shattered and cold. Soulless.

Instead, she was a light to those who lived in the darkness. A savior to the forgotten. She'd spent her life protecting the ones who couldn't save themselves.

In return, the creatures that she consorted with, the men and women of her life, used her and ignored her. They didn't care about her, didn't give her the respect and adoration that she deserved. If they had, they would have stopped hurting her so often.

He respected her. He adored her. He would never hurt her.

This was his gift to her. The body of a monster who had gotten to close to her, who had woven himself into her life. A gift from a man whom she'd never seen, never spoken to. A gift from the only one who truly understood her.

She was the only one who had experienced the monsters that lived in the darkness and come away unbroken, somehow stronger and brighter. This extraordinary humanity was what drew him to her and could be the key to his salvation.

Cassandra Matheson may not know him. But she would help him. She would fix the broken pieces inside of him because there was no one else who could. She would have to.

Or Cassandra Matheson would never escape her Cage.

Chapter 1

3 hours since the Cage, Age 31

Cassandra Matheson moaned as she rolled over. White sheets on a twin mattress? She had slate gray sheets on a king-sized bed. Where had these come from? And why did her head hurt so badly?

She rolled over and saw a room she had no memory of, furniture she'd never seen before. Panic began to fill her, heart racing as she assessed her situation. No sound left her lips, a habit long ago perfected. Cassandra never screamed from fear and never spoke without purpose. *Silence was safety*.

She'd been abducted.

Her body tensed as she stood up and realized that she had been stripped of her clothing. The simple flowery sun dress had been taken from her body when she'd been kidnapped. The air in the room was slightly cool on her tanned skin, but she shivered from fear rather than from the temperature.

Waves of terror rolled through her at the realization, but she closed her eyes and took deep breaths. Fear would not help her now. Only action and awareness. She surveyed her surroundings. The room was simple, not much different than a hotel room except that there was no window.

White painted drywall with a spackled texture flowed into a matching ceiling. A matching set of light oak furniture was all that was in the simple room. She moved to the set of drawers and began opening them, one by one. Emptiness was all that Cassandra found.

The oak nightstand did not hold a lamp as it would in a hotel, and there was no Bible in the drawers. A small writing desk and wooden chair sat in a corner. No decorations hung from the plain white walls. Inset lighting in the ceiling kept the room lit just as much as would be expected at any workplace.

It was a sterile environment. Nothing drew the eye. No one had used any of this. The floors were covered in a beige carpet that seemed to muffle the sound of her footsteps as she walked through the room.

In each of the four corners in the ceiling were cameras that followed her movements. She eyed them, knowing that they watched her move through the room completely naked. Fear may have been the surface emotion, but below everything else, anger bubbled, and it drove her to do more than shiver in fear.

No one would keep her in a cage. Never again.

Who had taken her? Why had they taken her? A man had held her, she remembered the hand. She gritted her teeth as the tiny memory came back. There were more than a handful of people who hated her, and most of them were terrible people.

Standing up, she knew that he watched her. He had already touched her, seen her naked body. Her captor would do what he wanted with her. She knew that. If he wanted to see her, she would not make it hard for him. *Submission was safety.*

This was not the first time that Cassandra had lived as a captive. It was not the first time that Cassandra had lived in fear of pain and suffering. She would survive. Regardless of anything else, Cassandra knew that she would survive. And she would find a way out.

What did he want? If he'd wanted to just cause her pain and torment, then why watch her? Why hadn't he strung her up and begun the torture already? If he'd wanted to rape her, why hadn't he had her tied to the bed? If he wanted her dead, why was she breathing still?

She had to understand her situation. She walked to the first door in the room. It was a simple door, wooden and white. Only a single thing made it different than a normal hotel room: there was no peephole.

She tried the door and found it locked. This was the way out. And the way in. This was where her captor would come from.

Cassandra tested the light switch next to the door, and the inset lighting in the ceiling went out no differently than a hotel room. The light from under the other door across the room was visible, but there was no light coming from under this one. That little bit of light from across the room was enough to see by. Almost like moonlight in a forest. It wasn't enough to see details, but enough to know that someone was there.

She moved to the door on the other side of the room. It swung open easily, and she found a fully stocked bathroom. The red light of a camera on two different corners followed her as she walked through the tiled hotel bathroom. Greens and blues filled the room, and though the colors should have brought some life to it, there was no life in this bathroom either. Again, just sterility.

The room was a cage. Her Cage. Everything was different in a cage, even the way that colors felt. The colors would never have the same brightness that they'd have if there had been a window in the room or a peep hole in the door. Freedom allowed colors and life, but this cage was filled with only darkness, filled with the nothingness that would slowly eat away at her mind.

She tested the water in the faucets and the shower. They worked. At least she'd be able to have the simple creature comforts of cleanliness and water when she wanted.

She walked back to the bedroom and sat back on the bed to contemplate what she would do.

Without making a sound, and without any warning, the lights went out. Not just the inset lighting in the ceiling. Every bit of light seemed to be stripped from the room. Pure darkness. She felt like she was standing in a cave without a light. Cassandra had been able to control herself when she could see, when she could understand what was happening, but this darkness was beyond anything she'd experienced.

She moved her hand in front of her face and could see nothing. No glint of movement or even a hope of seeing something. The hair on her arms felt the air change ever so slightly, and she heard something, a sound that she couldn't quite place. Then two soft thuds as something was set down.

The air changed again, almost as though there had been a brief wind in the room, and seconds of silence passed. The lights turned back on, blinding Cassandra for a few moments.

She looked around the room as her vision cleared and saw only two changes. A tray of food had been put on the desk. A simple sandwich and chips along with a glass of lemonade.

Beside the tray of food lay a notebook and a pencil. Cassandra went to inspect it. It was nothing special, just a simple spiral-bound notebook like a child would use in school.

He had been in the room. Only a few feet away from her. Somehow, he had been able to move through the darkness without any problem. Cassandra's heart pounded in her chest as she realized just how different this was to her previous cage. Once again, deep breaths helped to calm her panicked body.

The notebook waited on the desk as her body relaxed back into the alert but calm state she'd had before the lights had gone out. She picked it up and opened it to the first page.

Chapter 2

Cassandra,

I'm sure that you're wondering why you're here and where "here" is. The why is simple. I am… well, I'm a broken man, and I need you to help fix me. Psychologists would call me a psychopath, but most people would say that I'm soulless. I don't know what the truth is but let us say that I'm broken.

I've watched you for a long time, Cassandra Matheson. I've watched other people as well, but those experiments did not pan out. After years of thought and research, it is my opinion that you are the most likely person on the planet to teach me how to fix myself. The day that I 'feel' like other people is the day that I'll allow you to leave.

You have experienced the evils of the world, and you still try to help, still try to save the ones the world has forgotten. Unlike so many other people, when the world showed you the worst it had to offer, you did not break or lose your humanity.

All you have to do is show me how to be like you. Teach me, through these letters and through your actions, how to become more human, and I shall set you free. Teach me to feel something more than emptiness. That's all I ask. Until then, I have some rules.

Every day with your breakfast and your dinner, you'll receive this notebook and a letter from me. You are required to respond truthfully. I will not accept any lies, and I will know if you are lying.

If you follow the rules, you'll be rewarded. If you fail to follow the rules, you'll be punished.

My question: Why do you care so much? Why do you care about everyone else even when it makes things harder on you?

Chapter 3

12 hours before the Cage, Age 31

Cassandra leaned back in the ratty leather chair at her office. It had been a long week. She'd just moved back into her house after living in a hotel for the last two weeks. The police hadn't even tried to get the bloodstains out of her floor, so that had been the first thing she'd had to do when she'd gotten home. Rest just didn't come easily when your dining room still looked like a murder scene.

That wasn't even considering the difficulties at work. Regina had been working to get her children back, but she'd relapsed. Her kids had been excited, so excited to see their mom getting clean. But she'd lost her job, and instead of accepting a setback, she'd gone right back to the pipe to cope.

She hadn't shown up to her drug test, and she hadn't shown up to her court appointed therapy. It looked like she was going to have to start over again. Cassandra questioned why the courts allowed people like this to have second and third and fourth chances.

Cassandra was not a social worker for the parents. She was a child advocate first and foremost, and that would never change. Her upbringing wouldn't allow it. Life was hard on everyone, and if you were going to have children, you needed to take care of them. Your circumstances didn't decide whether you succeeded or not. It was the way you dealt with them that was important. Except when it came to children.

Children didn't have that freedom. They were forced to succumb to whatever hell their parents put them through. They couldn't fight their way out. They couldn't work or think or struggle through it. All they could do was survive. They didn't have the ability to leave their situation, and so it came down to social workers like Cassandra to be their escape.

Now, Cassandra closed her eyes to get a minute of peace. She'd just finished the paperwork to document all of Regina's failures. Cassandra's recommendation for the process to begin all over again would most likely make Regina give up on the hope of getting her kids back, but that was for the best. She'd seen the foster home they were in herself, and they were safe with foster parents who cared for their wards.

Her phone rang, breaking the silence of Cassandra's small office.

She looked down at her cell phone and saw that it was her boss, Mary Lancaster. Mary was a decent enough boss, but sometimes, she was more than a little clueless. Cassandra sighed.

"Hello Mary," she said, the frustration and exhaustion apparent in her voice.

"Cassandra, are you busy? I just got a call about a possible child abuse case, and the home is in your area."

Cassandra's case load came from a small suburb outside the city. It wasn't the town she'd grown up in, but it was similar enough. She knew what the people were like, and she knew what to look for.

"Who reported it?" Schools made things easy. Parents made things hard. Everywhere else was a crap shoot. No one wanted social workers around. In their eyes, social workers were worse than the police. They didn't take the bad guys away. They took the victims.

"A neighbor. He said that he heard multiple kids screaming." Mary hadn't been in the field in a long time. She'd forgotten to ask the right questions. What was normal? Were screaming kids normal? Was it silent typically? Were there pets? What about kids playing in the yard? What did the kids act like normally?

"Alright, Mary. I'll head over there. After that, I'm going to go home. It's been a long week."

"Text me when you finish up and let me know if you're picking up another case next week."

"Yes, ma'am," she said.

Cassandra hung up and packed her bag. She was tired. Probably too tired to be adding yet another case onto her already overloaded schedule. It didn't matter though. She was those kids' only advocate.

She carried her bag to her car and drove to the address Mary had texted her. The house was not one she'd have expected to have screaming kids or neighbors who reported it.

It was a two-story house with white paint and gray trim. Cassandra thought she could smell fresh paint as she stood on the porch. For a moment as she waited in front of the door, she had the glimmer of hope that the kids had screamed because of a scary movie or their parents playing a joke on them.

She brushed the wrinkles from the simple flowery sun dress she wore and took a deep breath. As she put her hand up to knock on the door, she heard a child's scream. High pitched and terrified. She knew the scream. This was not a scary movie scream. This was not a pain scream. This was true fear.

Cassandra was a social worker, and in a scenario where she believed a child was in danger, she had the legal right to enter any premise without a warrant or any other paperwork to assess the danger to the child. She took full advantage of that right as she turned the doorknob and rushed into the house.

She stopped unexpectedly as she looked at a "For Sale" sign sitting in an otherwise empty house. No furniture. No paintings. No people. Her heart raced as she looked around for the child who was terrified and saw a set of speakers connected to a phone on the ground.

Then she felt rough hands on her and a sharp stabbing pain in the side of her neck. It was only seconds before darkness overtook her and she collapsed.

Chapter 4

Captor,

Why do I care so much?

Why would I answer anything you ask me? You've abducted me and locked me in a Cage. Does the captured wolf owe its captor any loyalty?

You say that you want my help because you're broken. I've spent my life helping people who couldn't help themselves. Why wouldn't you just ask me for help? Why don't you simply talk to me like a human would?

I'll tell you why. You're not broken. You're a monster. Once upon a time, you may have been broken. A broken man asks for help, but that's not what you did. Instead, you've captured me and others before me. What did you do to them? Did you let them rot in this prison since they didn't provide you the answers you so desperately needed?

These are the acts of a monster, not a broken man. Whatever anyone else has told you, they're wrong. A psychopath does not ask for help. A soulless man does not wish to find humanity. Only a monster who was once a man would search for that shred of mankind still left in them.

Stop looking to other people for help. A monster need only look inside to find the man he once was. You will find no answers in me, and you will find no peace from atrocities you have committed. Stay in the dark, Monster, because the light will only show you how truly wretched you are.

Chapter 5

12 hours since the Cage, Age 31

Cassandra lay in the bed and stared at the wall. She'd slept for an unknown amount of time, the drugs making her more tired than normal. Now that she was awake again, thoughts ran through her mind, primarily about the note that she'd read and then her response back. Just as quickly, when she'd closed the notebook and sat back on the bed, the room had gone black, and the tray along with the journal had disappeared.

The sandwich had been good. Pastrami and sauerkraut on toast. Not a commonly eaten sandwich, but one that she was particularly fond of. She'd eaten it for as long as she could remember.

The most frustrating thing about the whole scenario was that she'd written her response in anger. She shouldn't have defied the Monster like that. She should have been more cooperative. The Monster had all the power, and she needed to remember to keep her anger in check. She'd known that. *Submission is safety.*

When she'd read that he wanted her help, it had pushed her past her normal calm demeanor and into pure anger. All he needed to do was ask her for help. She'd spent her life helping people. It was ridiculous to kidnap someone when a simple phone call would have sufficed.

Now… well, now she was stuck with the consequences of her anger. She did not look forward to whatever punishment the Monster would decide on. At the same time, she knew that whatever the punishment was, she would survive it.

The lights shut off again, and Cassandra shivered in the dark, afraid of the coming blow, of the monster that may appear when the lights came back on. She didn't know who or what lay in the darkness, and that unknown was terrifying. She had dealt with her fair share of monsters, and when you pulled them from the darkness and into the light, they were rarely as frightening as your mind thought them to be.

But when the soft wind blew, and the lights came back on with blinding intensity, there was no monster. Even after her letter, after she had defied the Monster, no punishment awaited her. She looked to the desk, to see what was for breakfast and she saw an opened can and a fork next to it.

She stood up and walked the short distance to the desk, knowing quickly what it was that she had been given for her breakfast. An opened can of wet cat food lay next to the journal. The smell of something that might have been mistaken as fish rose from the tin can.

"I guess that I'm going to go hungry this morning," she said under her breath as she slid the can to the back of the desk. The journal lay on the table next to the pencil, and Cassandra felt her heart rate speed up.

This notebook, and these letters were strange. They reminded her of something, but she couldn't put her finger on it. The thought passed, and she sat down at the desk. She opened the journal.

Chapter 6

Cassandra,

You didn't ask a single question, but they all kind of turned into one. "Why didn't I just call you and ask you to help?"

Well, that would be a good question except that you'd never help me. I am not a child. I am not helpless. I am not a lost soul that you can relate to. At least not on a surface level. Even if you had cared about me, you wouldn't have personally helped me.

You'd have sent me to some psychologist to puzzle out my issues with them. Trust me, I've seen enough psychologists and psychiatrists that I highly doubt any you could find would tell me something new. If I could have given you a call and expected to resolve my problems, I would have already done that.

No amount of drugs or talking to therapists will resolve my problem. I'm missing a soul, Cassandra. I'm broken beyond repair. Except by you. Possibly.

I have abducted you. I do not plan on hurting you as long as you follow the rules. I am keeping my identity secret purposefully. That way, I can take you home when you're done helping me. I hope that this spurs you to productive motion instead of frustratingly annoying stubbornness. I do not wish to punish you, but I will do what I must do to achieve my goals. Which brings me to the next topic.

I hope you enjoy your breakfast. I bought the expensive stuff. It says gourmet on the can, so you know it's good. I was tempted to mix it into something so that you'd accidentally eat it without knowing what to expect, but I decided against it on the offhand chance that you just thought I was a bad cook.

If you continue to act like an animal in a cage rather than my guest, I will treat you like it. The human food will go away, and I will show you just how much of a monster I can be as I watch you finally cave and eat from a can of cat food as hunger pains force you to ignore your disgust.

Now, that can of cat food is not a punishment. That is a warning. I am very serious about how this game is played. You are my captive until I am satisfied, and you should be glad that I am willing to play this game with complete honesty. You can ask whatever question you'd like, but I warn you, if you ask my identity, I will tell you, and that will mean that I can never release you.

You also only get one question per letter. This game will be a long one, so get comfortable. The best way to prevent this from being too miserable is to keep answering questions as honestly and as completely as possible, and I will do my best to provide you with rewards to take the tedium out of your day.

My question to you: What's your favorite book?

Chapter 7

27 years before the Cage, Age 4

Smoke was everywhere. The child, Cassandra, was staring at the smoke that curled up from under the door. Her lips were painted an ashy gray. The air was orange inside the home, and paint had begun peeling from the heat.

Four years old, the small child's tears were streaking through powdered ash that built up on her cheeks. No cries came from her lips, but the smoke caused her eyes to water. Her parents were nowhere to be seen, and the brown-haired girl was all alone.

A man wearing striped pajama pants and no shirt or shoes broke into the room, slamming the door open. His eyes darted around the room, taking in everything with the single glance. He said nothing as he ran through the smoke and picked the little girl up. Ignoring pieces of the walls cracking under the licking tongues of flame, he rushed the two of them out of the house and to safety on the sidewalk outside their suburban home.

The man was Cassandra's neighbor, a good man who had drank beers with her father and let his own daughter play with Cassandra.

She'd known him and would forever remember him as the one who had saved her, who had been *her* advocate. He'd rushed outside and stood facing the street while he held Cassandra over his shoulder. He spoke in a panic to his wife. The stairway to the second story was on fire and he couldn't get up.

A loud crash filled the air as something collapsed inside the house. Smoke was everywhere, curling up higher than Cassandra could see. The flames inside of the house were filling the windows with an orange glow.

Cassandra kept watching a single window. The window to her parents' bedroom. She didn't know where her parents were.

The fire department had already been called, and they'd be there any minute. You could hear them in the distance, but her neighbor kept saying that they had to get Cassandra's parents out.

Then Cassandra saw them. Her mother and father were at the window. They were wrestling with the window. Cassandra smiled at them and tried to wave, but they didn't see her. The house was older, and the windows sometimes got stuck in the summers from the humidity.

Her neighbor didn't see it happen. His wife didn't either. The only person in the world to witness the collapsing roof and the death of her parents was Cassandra. Only she saw the walls collapse and fall inward as flames rushed into the night air. Only she saw the sparks fly as her parents were crushed. Only she watched as the last people in her life were burned to death.

The four-year-old girl didn't cry. She just stared at the empty placed that had been her parents' bedroom, capturing the moment in her memory for the rest of her life.

Chapter 8

Dear Captor,

My favorite book is The Count of Monte Cristo. It has a little bit of everything, action and adventure, love, and revenge. The revenge may end up becoming a little more intense than would be necessary for most, but in my opinion, anyone who tries to ruin your life should be punished in a similar fashion.

I question whether that's the best 'favorite' book. The correlation between it and my current situation is difficult to deny. Maybe I should have chosen The Littlest Unicorn Who Shits Rainbows as my favorite? Then I could be frolicking in a field with a rainbow shitting unicorn instead of in a cell. Too late for the change in taste, I guess.

I apologize for my anger yesterday. I am sure that you understand my frustration at being locked in a cell for an unknown amount of time. I will try to maintain a calmer demeanor.

What is your favorite book?

Chapter 9

2 days since the Cage, Age 31

It had been two days since Cassandra had been captured and brought to her cage. Two days of nothing except the letters at breakfast and dinner. Dinner should be coming soon. At least that was what Cassandra thought. She had done nothing except lay in bed, and time becomes strange in a cage with no window to the outside world.

It was time to get out of bed. She could smell herself. A shower would help her wake up and maybe see something she'd missed in her assessment of her Cage.

As she thought about taking a shower, she thought about the cameras following her every move. She had been surprised that the Monster had not done anything sexual to her after taking away her clothes and leaving her naked in the room.

Why else would her clothes have been taken away? She got up and walked to the bathroom. She looked at the camera in the corner. She'd been annoyed at them when she had needed to use the toilet, but like everything here, it was smarter to simply comply. She tried to maintain the calm and collected mental state that would let her survive until she found a way to escape.

She opened the glass shower door and turned on the shower, letting the steam start before she got inside and began to wash herself. A can of shaving cream and a razor lay inside the shower. That made Cassandra laugh to herself. She wouldn't let herself become covered in filth, but she wasn't about to get sexy for Monster.

There was something about showers that made them scary places to be in when there were monsters about. She had spent the last two days knowing there was a monster on the other side of the door, and she'd been nervous. Standing in the glass shower was different somehow, and every time she closed her eyes, her heart began to race.

Eventually, she stopped closing her eyes and stared at the door to the bathroom while she washed herself. The fear of being caught unprepared in the shower was too much for her.

As she finished rinsing off, the lights turned off. She'd been right. It was dinner. She didn't move, her hand still on the knob to turn off the water. She didn't move at all and didn't make a sound.

But in the darkness, even over the noise of the shower she heard a soft scratching like claws on metal. It was an animal, a small one, and it puzzled her. The lights came back on, and she turned off the shower.

Not having a towel didn't bother her. It wasn't her floor that she was tracking water through. She walked through the room, and she saw that in addition to her dinner and the journal, there was a cage set on her bed.

The cage was small, and as she approached it, Cassandra began to laugh. Inside was a white striped orange kitten no bigger than her hand. It was pouncing on a cotton mouse, and as Cassandra opened the cage door, it hissed at her and tried to swat her with its paw.

Cassandra grinned at the little creature and pulled it out of the cage. She picked up the cage in her other hand and brought it to a corner out of the way before sitting down with the ferocious beast who still carried the mouse in its mouth. The cat's claws were barely long or sharp enough to pierce the skin, but that didn't stop it from doing its best to murder her.

She put it on the bed and watched it begin to stalk her hand as it carried the mouse with it. She played with the fluffball for several minutes, enjoying the way that he refused to let her win. In his mind, even though he was the size of a mouse, Cassandra was the prey. Cassandra finally sighed and put the cat down on the ground.

She needed to take a look at the journal, but first, it was time to eat. A turkey breast, mashed potatoes, and green beans. She looked at her food and then realized that she didn't have any food for the kitten.

And so, she began to cut part of the turkey breast into bite sized pieces for the little cat. "If I'm going to give you my food, you need a name, beast," she said as he ran around her feet, pouncing and biting before rushing off. She couldn't help but smile every time he tried his best to attack her.

She carried the pieces of turkey breast in one hand, and she snatched up the cat in the other. He snarled and tried to scratch her hand the entire time that she held him. Luckily, his claws were still small enough to be cute. She carried them both into the bathroom and put the turkey pieces onto the tile floor, and then she sat the kitten next to the pieces. It immediately began to eat. Any time she put her hand near the food, the kitten hissed and attacked her.

"I'd call you Tiger for how ferocious you are, but you're too little. How about Tigger?" Cassandra smiled at it and went back to her own food. It was a good, hearty meal, but she was left a little hungry.

Finally, when the food was done, she turned her attention to the journal.

Chapter 10

Cassandra,

    I appreciate the apology. I understood your frustration, and that is why I didn't punish you for breaking the rules.

    I hope you enjoy the kitten. I know that you've spent your life taking care of others, so I wanted to make sure that you had someone to take care of. It's a ferocious beast. Watch your toes.

    Maybe it would have been better for both of us if we'd had different tastes. Though I have my doubts about unicorns being as gentle and sweet as the stories try to make them out to be. They're magical horses, and anyone who's spent time around horses knows that there are plenty of them who are assholes. The last thing I'd want is to 'frolic' with an asshole with a horn and magic powers.

    My favorite book is Alice in Wonderland. It's the last book that my mother read me before she died when I was six. That nostalgia, and those memories are some of the strongest memories I have of my childhood. Most of the rest of it is a blur of nothingness.

    Beyond the memory, I connect with the book. The way she wanders through Wonderland surprised by every person and creature she meets was how I lived as a child. I never understood the reason why people did the things they did. The bad people were hurtful for reasons I could never understand, and the good ones were often hurt because they were kind.

    None of it made sense to me as a child, and to this day, I sometimes become confused at why people do the things they do.

I'll give you my question as an example of my confusion. "Why would you continue to date a man who was fucking another woman?"

Chapter 11

21 days before the Cage, Age 31

W ine flowed like an unending river that night. Victoria and Alexis, Cassandra's two best friends, sat on her couch on the second bottle of the night. Alexis, a thin woman of Greek descent, had been dumped. Her fiancé had decided that he was unhappy with their sex life, and that it was impossible for them to work through that.

Cassandra had decided to hold a night of debauchery to celebrate Alexis's freedom from a man who had never been worth her time. The TV was currently on some movie about male strippers, and Victoria was talking about how Alexis was better off without her fiancé.

"It's not you, Alexis. Every man complains about his girlfriend's lack of sex drive. It's complete bullshit, you know that, right? I mean, being tired and not wanting some guy grunting and sweating on top of you while they completely ignore whether you're turned on or not just isn't something that we should have to put up with. Like, that's pretty damn close to rape, you know? Guys shouldn't be able to break up with you just because we don't want them to rape us. It's bullshit."

Cassandra raised an eyebrow at the mention of rape. "I don't think that's actually rape, Victoria."

Alexis just kept drinking while Victoria replied, "Well, you know what I mean. It may not be rape, but it's damn sure close enough. If he loved you like you deserve, he wouldn't have quit the relationship just because you didn't want him to kind of rape you."

"Victoria, it's not rape. It's not even close to rape. It's annoying, but it's not rape." Cassandra had the hint of a smile on her lips as she sipped her wine much slower than her partners in crime.

"It *was* annoying," Alexis said as she stared drunkenly at the men dancing around the screen in thongs. "But it was more than that. He wanted me to do things that I didn't want to do. He said that I should try anal because he wanted to. He... he said I didn't love him enough if I wouldn't even try it. Maybe it *was* kind of like rape."

"It wasn't rape because you could say no, and you did say no," Cassandra said softly. "It wasn't good, but it wasn't rape. There's a difference, and you shouldn't ignore it or brush aside the difference because you want to be dramatic. That doesn't make him a good guy, Alexis, but it doesn't make him a rapist."

"I guess that's true," Victoria said, the mood in the room suddenly much more somber.

"He was fat though," Cassandra said with a smile on her face. "Now you don't have to marry a fat guy."

Alexis laughed out loud at her sudden outburst. Victoria snarled a little bit. She had a few pounds that she'd like to lose. "He really has gotten fat, hasn't he?"

"He's a porker, Alexis, and you're fucking hot. Maybe if he hadn't been such a porker, you'd have wanted to fuck him more often." Cassandra had a sparkle in her eye now, and the girls were on a roll again.

As the laughs dried up a little, Alexis turned to Cassandra. "What about you, Cassandra?" Alexis asked. "Has Craig ever tried to get you to do stuff you don't want to do? Like anal?"

"He still tries. He pushes and pushes, but you know what? If he's going to leave me over butt sex, he's going to leave me over something eventually. So, I hold my ground, and I don't let people bully me. Especially not the guy I'm supposed to love."

She took a sip of her wine before continuing. "It's fucking annoying though. Some days, I wish I had a dick so I could tell him that I'd let him put it in my ass if I could put it in his first."

Victoria immediately rolled out of her chair in a fit of laughter. "Could you imagine Craig getting fucked in the ass by Cassandra? I bet you'd have a big dick, Cassandra. Maybe I'll get you a strap-on for your next birthday or maybe an anniversary?" Alexis said, a smile creeping onto her face.

"Maybe we should all get strap-ons for when the inevitable conversation happens. Then again," Cassandra said with a half-smile, "what if they like it? Then they'd expect us to do all the work, and they'd want to fuck our asses too. That'd be terrible."

More laughter as they all began to come up with more and more ridiculous ways to stave off the question of anal.

Chapter 12

Dear Captor,

Craig, my boyfriend, only cheated once, and I forgave him. Men do stupid things. They are ruled by their cocks, and other than the single transgression, Craig had done nothing else that could be considered cheating.

If you're trying to understand people, you should know that they rarely are as simple as you'd expect if all you do is watch them. Sure, you can see a woman go to the same coffee shop every morning and drink the same coffee as she shoots glances at a man who works there.

If you were to assume that she had a crush on him, you may be correct. But you could also be very wrong. She could be missing her brother who was fighting overseas and looked like him, or maybe he would be the same age as her best friend who died. Her motivation could be anything.

Don't assume things about people. Just because someone cheats once doesn't mean that they're still cheating. Just because Craig made a mistake doesn't mean that he continued to make mistakes. People learn, and people grow. Don't assume, and you'll rarely make mistakes when judging people.

My question to you, oh great and powerful Captor, "Why do you think he was still cheating?"

Cassandra Matheson

Chapter 13

5 days since the Cage, Age 31

The cat pounced on her toes through the blanket. Morning was here again. Cassandra wiggled her toes and let the creature attack them again. She tapped the kitten's nose with her big toe, and he backed up, his ears flattened against his head, tail twitching, and his fur sticking up. Cassandra smiled as she wiggled her toes again, and the little beast pounced, biting and scratching at it.

She pulled her feet to her, snuggling up to the blanket. She'd become accustomed to her imprisonment at this point. The worry that Monster would come for her, to bring pain or something else more sinister, was still there, but it was far less pressing. The routine had been established, and she'd spent her time playing with the kitten.

The beast was a terror. No doubt, this little murderer would grow up to be a fat house cat eventually, but for now, it lived only to attack her feet or any other part of her that was exposed. Biting and tearing at her with his tiny little razor blade claws had left Cassandra's skin with thin red lines where he'd attacked.

Suddenly, in the midst of biting her toe through the blanket, the kitten stopped. Its ears swiveled, listening intently, and Cassandra didn't move. There was a noise, a rumbling, coming from outside her walls. Someone or something was outside the building, and Cassandra listened closely. Her ears followed the sound, but her eyes followed the cameras.

She stood up, and the cat did not follow. Its ears continued to swivel as it tried to understand the new noise. She walked across the room, and though her ears continued to listen to the rumbling, her eyes watched the cameras to see if they followed her. As she walked to the bathroom, the cameras continued to stay stationary.

Maybe there isn't anyone watching, she thought. She walked back to the bed. Without trying to be sneaky, she crawled under the bed. If someone was watching, they would see her. If they weren't, then the faster she got under the bed, the quicker she would be done.

It was on the second day of her captivity that she had realized any escape attempt would have to come from under the bed. It was the only place that was hidden from the cameras. She hadn't known what her escape attempt would entail, but knowing what puzzle pieces one has is half the process to solving the puzzle.

She lay on her stomach under the bed, the kitten still on top of the bed. If this worked out, she'd be sad to leave the cat, but there was nothing to be done about it. The damn thing would never have let her carry it through an escape.

The rumbling was still a low drone in the background. Whatever was causing it was still there. She began to scratch fiercely at the drywall. It took a bit of effort to scratch through the paint, but once that was gone, the drywall crumbled quickly.

The space between studs would be plenty large enough to walk through. If it was a normal house, all that she had to do to escape her cage was to scratch her way through the drywall. She would have just punched the wall, but the fear of hitting a stud and hurting her hand dissuaded that idea.

Finally, she was through the drywall, but instead of the open space she'd hoped to find, she felt something hard and very rough. She peeled a larger chunk of drywall off the wall and let it fall, revealing a gray brick.

Fuck.

She looked at the cinderblock and realized that there would be no tunneling through the walls. Maybe if she could steal a spoon or a knife, she could dig through the blocks.

The real problem with that was that the Monster watched her nearly constantly. She'd seen the cameras follow her movements consistently throughout her time, and it was only the intrusion that had allowed her the moment away from his watchful gaze. Night or day, it didn't matter. There was never a definite time that the cameras would not follow her movements, and that meant that the Monster watched her night and day.

She rolled back out from under the bed and crawled under the sheets again. She needed a plan. She looked at the door and wondered how she could manage an escape attempt when there was no way to catch the Monster off guard.

She could try to break down the door by using the chair on it. Maybe it would break, but after seeing the cinder blocks, she doubted that it was a cheap door that would fail from her hitting it with a chair. More likely, she would break the chair and then she'd be punished.

She laid back in the bed, extremely frustrated at how well her captor had planned this. Every cage has a weak point, though, and all she had was time. She could cause a disturbance, do something that would force the Monster into the cell, but he could somehow see in the darkness, and she couldn't. That was really the biggest advantage he had. He could see her, and she couldn't see him.

What if she didn't need to see him? What if she made that difference go away? And as soon as the lights went out, he didn't have the cameras to know where she was anymore. Blind people functioned all the time, so why couldn't she do the same thing? Why couldn't she memorize her room and learn to move without sight? The space was small enough to learn.

She smiled to herself. For the first time since she had been captured, Cassandra Matheson had a plan.

And then the lights went out. Complete and utter darkness, just like every other time. As she slid her foot across the bed, she felt Tigger's furry little body, and he lashed out, biting and scratching her foot again.

The pain was strange in the darkness. It hurt more because her mind couldn't comprehend exactly what was happening. It was like taste without smell. What does a chocolate cake taste like if you can't smell it at all?

She hissed at the cat, and for the first time, it stopped and moved away, the lack of sight making it less courageous. She knew the Monster was only a few feet away, probably close enough that if they both reached out, that they would touch. It didn't matter though. She was frozen. The darkness would not allow her to move.

If she was going to succeed at this, she would need to learn to move without the light. She would need to learn to stop being afraid of the darkness.

Then the lights came back on, and she blinked the blindness away. On the bed next to her sat the clothes that she'd been wearing when she'd been abducted, laundered and neatly folded. He'd been close enough to touch. His hand had come within inches of her body.

Her mind took in the information, and she tried to remember if she'd heard anything, even something as small as that bit of wind that signaled the door was opening. Nothing she could remember. She would have to learn to pay more attention.

She looked at Tigger and smiled. She had a practice buddy at least. She could figure it all out later. For now, her and Tigger needed to eat, and as always, she had her letter. She got out of bed and picked up the clothes. She put on the simple, yet elegant black bra and panties.

Cassandra Matheson was a woman who was always prepared. She didn't buy things because they were cute. She bought them for a purpose, and underwear, in her opinion at least, should always be both sexy and comfortable.

She slid the flowery sun dress on after that. After the long days and nights of nudity, it was strange to put clothes back on. Other people would have been overjoyed to be able to cover up when they knew that someone was watching, but Cassandra had gotten over the watched feeling.

He wouldn't stop watching, and if her nudity had been something that he'd been interested in, he wouldn't have given her clothes back. At least they would protect her from the kitten's teeth and claws. She gave it a grin and shook her fingers at the beast. It reared back on its hind legs as it tried to pounce.

She sat down at the desk and looked at her breakfast. Four sausage links, eggs, and toast with raspberry jam, her favorite flavor. She carried the plate to the bathroom. Tigger followed her, knowing exactly what was happening. She scooped half the eggs onto the bathroom floor and the kitten began to gobble them up. She scooted her foot closer to him, and he tried to scratch her.

"You little beast. Don't you know that those are my eggs that you're eating?" The cat didn't respond, and she shook her head as she walked back to the desk. She wasn't all that concerned about the letter that waited for her, but she was starving.

Two meals a day was not enough food for her, and she was giving part of her protein to the cat every meal. It wasn't enough to make her starve, but it was enough of a difference to notice.

She ate silently. The only time she talked anymore was when she was talking to the cat. The clothes had been a reward for following the rules. She knew that. They hadn't been a reward for her even though she was sure that most people would have thought that they'd been one.

The cat, though, was a very different kind of reward. He was a reward that Cassandra could appreciate. He had provided the only entertainment that she'd experienced since waking up in the Cage. Yet, he wasn't just entertainment. He was a reminder that there was life even in her Cage.

As Cassandra opened the journal to look at the newest letter from the Monster, she looked down at the cat who was meowing loudly below her. She put the plate on the ground and let the kitten lick up all the rest of the crumbs.

Chapter 14

Cassandra,

I didn't assume anything. Craig told me that he'd been cheating on you. He told me in explicit detail how and when he'd cheated on you.

The difference between us is that I understand how people act when they're strapped to a table while you hold a knife above them. You've never experienced how they act. You've never listened to them respond when you ask them a question as a blade slides across their flesh.

If I had asked Craig about his cheating while we were drinking a beer, I would not have been able to tell if he was lying. That's the problem with most people. Unless they're stressed, it's difficult to tell when they're lying or telling the truth. Pain is the ultimate motivator.

I asked Craig about the woman he was fucking after I'd flayed the skin from each of his fingers. He'd already found that lying made the pain worse. I'm sure that you remember finding the fingers on the floor beside his body. He lost a finger after he told the truth to each of the answers.

The first finger, well, all of the flesh was gone from that one before he finally told the truth. It took nearly an hour to coax the truth of the matter out of him. An hour to strip bit after bit of skin from his finger as he screamed. He hadn't understood the game well enough at that time. The second finger had still taken quite a bit of flesh to come to the truth. It took many lies, and a lot of screaming.

You'd be interested to know that when I asked him about you on the eighth finger, he didn't hesitate to tell me all about your schedule. He already knew that I was going to kill him. I'd told him over and over again that death was his only escape from the pain. By the time that we were talking about you, he was begging for death, begging for the pain to end.

Yet, when it came to questions about you, he didn't protect you. He didn't hesitate. I knew the answers already of course, so you shouldn't blame him for your captivity, but it is interesting that the man who slept in your bed every night was willing to give up your safety because of a bit of pain.

By the last finger, he was telling me what I wanted to know before I had even drawn blood. By the time I held his pinky finger and held up the knife, he didn't hesitate. I'm sure that you hadn't looked closely, but that last pinky finger hadn't been flayed at all.

Ten fingers, and ten truths. Eight of them were answers I already knew. Eight of them were tests. He told me lie after lie initially, but as I said, pain is the ultimate motivator of a man.

By the time that he told me about how he'd been inside of Victoria a week prior, he'd already given up lying. He told me every detail he could think of. He told me about how she enjoyed the way he fucked her, how she was so glad to think he was choosing her over you. He even told me how he was just doing it because he was bored.

He told me about the way she begged him to be rough. He told me about the way that she had sucked him after he'd fucked her. He told me that he never regretted it at all.

All of that was after he'd already told me how you never turned him down, how you let him follow his most depraved fantasies. Once again, I wonder about you, wonder about how you could let a man so worthless use you like that and then forgive him for lying to you. Even if you believed it was only the one time. Was it because he was that good in bed?

It's too bad that people don't answer more truthfully without being motivated. I'm sure that life would be simpler and less painful for everyone if we all just spoke the truth. Don't you think?

That wasn't my question. Please don't think that I'm breaking my own rules. Rhetoricals don't count because they don't require an answer and still make the same point.

Regardless, I believe that I've answered your question sufficiently. Let's talk about something a little less macabre. I hope that you enjoy the clothing. I appreciate the truthfulness that you've shown me, and if there are things that you believe would help alleviate the inevitable tedium of being here, please let me know.

I may have trapped you, but I'd prefer it if your captivity was as pleasant as possible. I know that a cage is a boring place.

My question is, "How did finding Craig's body in your dining room make you feel?"

Chapter 15

"Yes Mary, I can take care of it tomorrow." Cassandra said as she put her key into the door of her apartment.

"Thanks, Cassandra. I'll see you then."

"Okay. See you later." She hung up the phone and put it into her pocket as she turned the doorknob.

"Craig. I'm home." She said loudly. She closed the door and walked through her entryway. She set her purse down on the metal-framed walnut credenza. The living room was dark. She wondered where her boyfriend Craig was as she walked through the living room without bothering to turn on the light.

Her sensible black heels tapped softly in the silence of her three-bedroom home as she walked, the only sound. When she got into the kitchen, she stopped. The lights were off in this room as well. What was going on?

Drip. Drip. Drip.

It was like the sink faucet was leaking, but softer. No echo. She glanced at the sink. There was no drip. Maybe it was coming from the bathroom?

She walked into the dining room, and she stopped, her body freezing in place.

Craig lay face up on her dining room table. One arm hung over the side of the table, and a puddle of blood lay under it. Ten blood covered fingers lay in the puddle under the hand.

Drip. Drip. Drip.

She watched as the blood dripped off his hand where his pinky finger should have been, a trail running down his arm from his shirt which had once been a bright yellow and was now crimson.

Cassandra didn't scream or cry out as she stared at him and tried to comprehend what she was seeing. She'd seen a lot of things in her life. More than anyone she'd ever met. This was the first time she'd seen a dead body, though.

It was a surreal thing to see that river of red so dark that it almost looked black. Her eyes lost their focus as she stared.

Anyone who knew Cassandra would know that she wouldn't have screamed. She wasn't a screamer. That had been beaten out of her. She'd learned long ago that *silence was safety*. Whoever had killed her boyfriend could still be there.

She stepped backward, slowly, doing her best to not make a noise. She grabbed her purse and keys from the credenza. Her body moved without thought as she unlocked her car and got inside. The engine roared to life, and she drove away. *Distance was safety.*

Chapter 16

Captor,

You're the one who killed Craig? You're the one who tortured him? What the fuck is wrong with you? Why would you think that was okay? And why the fuck would you tell me?

Was it because he was cheating? That isn't an excuse. I would have forgiven him. He may not have been the best boyfriend, but I've been with worse ones. He didn't hit me. He didn't make me feel afraid. He was pretty, and he made me laugh. And yes, he was very good in bed.

Were you jealous? That would make a lot more sense to me. You've followed me around, pretending to understand me. You see me and Craig together, and then you decide to kill him so that you can convince me to fall in love with you. That sounds about right for a psychopath monster.

Now you want to know how it made me feel? What kind of fucked up individual kills someone, captures their girlfriend, and then asks that kind of question? It made me want to cry. It made me want to scream and throw things. It made me afraid enough that I didn't sleep in my own bed for two weeks.

Are you still fucking learning from me? Are you still wanting me to teach you how to feel? Here's my first lesson. Don't fucking kill people if you want their significant other to help you.

My question is "Why in the fuck did you kill him?"

Chapter 17

5 days since the Cage, Age 31

Cassandra woke up groggily. Something had happened. Something was different. She tried to wipe the sleep away from her eyes, but her hand wouldn't move correctly. She tried to sit up and realized that her hands and legs were bound to the bed.

She also realized that all of her clothes were gone. The blanket was gone, and the kitten was nowhere to be seen. From the bathroom, she heard a soft repetitive meowing.

Cassandra's legs were tied in such a way that she was fully exposed. Her feet had been tied with rope to her thighs, and her thighs had been tied to the bed frame, forcing her body into a completely open position. She pulled on her bindings, testing them one by one. She took deep breaths to calm her body as panic began to fill it.

She looked at a camera, acknowledging the man behind the lens. He had drugged her again. Drugged her and bound her body to the bed. She'd been so angry when she'd read his letter.

Once again, she'd let her anger control her actions. She'd let her anger fill the page, flowing from one damning comment to the next. Anger was the one emotion that she'd never been able to keep under control.

Now the Monster was showing her just how he dealt with an angry captive. She was spread for him. He'd already admitted to killing a man and kidnapping her. Did she really think that he would be opposed to raping her for her insolence? Was that what he'd meant by punishments?

The lights shut off, and Cassandra was left terrified. Her body tensed, preparing itself for the inevitable violation. The darkness meant only one thing. He was coming into the room.

The room was silent other than the kitten in the bathroom. Cassandra tried to calm herself. It was just rape. Just rape. That was all. He needed her. He needed her to teach him. She would survive.

The wind blew just enough for her hair to move.

Her legs pulled against her bonds once again, this time in hopes that she could break them or move out of them somehow. There were no flaws in the Monster's knots. She would not be leaving her bondage unless he allowed it.

Her breath came out in soft pants as she tried to get a grip on her body's instincts. She knew she had no choice in whatever happened at this point. There was nothing she could do to prevent it. Nothing she could do to stop him from doing whatever he wanted with her body.

"What do you want? My body? My fear? My pain?" She panted harder and fear crept past her normally logical and controlled mind.

"I won't be able to teach you anything if you hurt me." Cassandra's hands pulled as hard as she could against the ropes. She heard the rope strain against her. She knew she was lying. If he hurt her, he could still force her to do things. As he'd said, pain was the ultimate motivator.

Then she heard a sound. Softer than she'd expected. A whispered breath. Not a voice, not a noise. Just the wind passing by a monster's lips. Just an unnatural wind an inch away from her body, an inch away from her breast.

Sexual desire was part of it. Part of whatever drove this monster. It had to be. Otherwise, why would he be this close, this inquisitive. She could almost feel the heady desire coming off whoever was standing over her prone body.

She shivered. Terrified of the creature that held her captive. Terrified of what he might do. Her mind ran through scenes of possible torment that he could inflict on her bound body. Maybe it wouldn't just be rape.

She knew pain. She knew how to deal with it, but at the same time, she was beginning to believe that the monster knew how to cause it better than any of her previous nightmares had.

Then the wind came again. The second one meant the door had shut and the monster was gone. Why had he left? Why *hadn't* he raped her or tortured her?

Time passed strangely as the lights stayed off. She'd thought she could handle the darkness. She'd thought it would be like being blind, like closing her eyes, but it was different. Even when you closed your eyes as tight as you could, there was still the smallest amount of light getting through. This was different.

She'd gotten used to her life in the Cage. She'd felt comfortable. There had been worse cages. Cages without toilets. Cages without her kitten. Cages without food.

The darkness was something she'd never experienced, and it was like every second of it was exhausting and terrifying. Her body trembled even as Cassandra tried to calm it.

Nothingness. That's what was so terrifying in this new dimension to her Cage. The only thing that pulled her back from madness was the soft meowing of her kitten. Now that her body was on high alert, she heard the little beast scratching softly at the plastic bottom of his cage in between meows.

He wouldn't give up on escape. Even in the darkness, Cassandra closed her eyes and took another breath. Even a kitten knew that you couldn't give up just because the cage felt unbreakable. She couldn't give up either. She'd had a plan this morning.

She would not let the nothingness keep her from her plan. No matter what her captor tried to do, she would do everything she could to get out of the Cage.

She closed her eyes and let the time pass in darkness.

Chapter 18

Cassandra,

I thought it was obvious why I killed Craig. He was taking advantage of you, and you refused to leave. I knew that even if I showed you that he was cheating, you wouldn't leave him. He wasn't good for you. He had to go.

I could have done other things. I could have shown you his history of cheating. I could have shown you better men, or I could have even just scared him away. I've tried to help you in the past like this, but you rarely follow the pushes that I give you. I decided that this would be far simpler and far more effective.

You've spent your life doing good for everyone. You've given pieces of yourself to each of them, just as you give your food to that cat. The cat cannot help you. It will never be able to help you to escape. It won't feed you if I take your food away.

That kitten, and every child you have saved from monsters owes you their lives. They'll never be able to repay you. They'll never give you anything or help you in any way. Yet, you continue to help them.

Craig saw this selflessness. He didn't return the goodness that you deserved. Instead, he just took advantage it, of your ability to forgive. He did not deserve you, and he would have hurt you until someone forced him to stop.

He was my gift to you, no different than a kitten would bring you a dead mouse. It's interesting that you would praise the cat for killing vermin, yet you are angry at me for doing the same simply because he was human and could lie to you.

If you must be angry at someone for killing him, I will let that anger fall on my shoulders. They are strong enough to carry even that burden, but I could not watch that creature crawl into bed with you a single night longer. He was not worthy of you, and he would never have become worthy.

You have done too much good for too many people for anyone to have allowed that man to continue to stay in your life. One day, I hope that you will understand my reasoning and that the anger will fade.

For now, I will accept that your anger is the cost of your safety. I had once thought that you would learn to protect yourself from those that would hurt you, but I have watched you for too long to be deluded. You're not some ignorant teen. You should have learned to protect yourself long ago, but instead, you seem bound and determined to let the creatures of the world succeed in breaking you.

My question must veer away from our current discussion, though. "Why did you lie about your last answer?" You were not sad. I did not see you cry even once. You were not sad, and that is a lie. That is why you were punished today. I did not want to punish you, but it was necessary to remind you that there are rules, and you must follow them.

Chapter 19

"Ya have to go with 'em, Cassandra," Miss Faith said softly. A tear fell down her cheek as she knelt in front of the 5-year-old brown haired little girl.

"But… but… Miss Faith, why can't ya keep me? I promise I won't do nothin' wrong again. I promise!" Cassandra looked up at the woman as she pleaded with her. Her eyes were filled with sadness.

"You didn't do nothin' wrong, sweetheart." Miss Faith gave Cassandra a big hug as she let more tears fall.

"Then why do I have to go? Why can't ya keep me? I don't care if you don't got no moneys. You're nice. Really nice. There's other ma's and pa's out there that ain't so nice, Miss Faith. Please don't make me go!"

"Honey, I don't want ya to go, but we can't be foster parents if the gov'ment is givin' us housing assistance. Big Tony lost his job, and my hip don't let me work."

Cassandra looked down at the ground. This was her third foster home in a year and a half since her parents had died. Her first two foster parents had been ill-equipped to take care of a girl like Cassandra.

No one had understood her like Miss Faith and Big Tony had. Cassandra looked at Miss Faith. "Why not?"

Miss Faith picked Cassandra up with a grimace. Her hip had needed a replacement for almost twenty years, but there hadn't ever been the money or the time. The arthritis had started when she was thirty, far younger than most, but now that she was fifty, there was no cartilage left. It was a wonder that she could get out of bed most days.

She held the child to her shoulder as she rocked her. Cassandra was too old to be held like this, but that didn't matter to either of them. Cassandra hadn't been held for six months before she'd been placed with Miss Faith and Big Tony. It had been hard on her.

"Them's the rules, girl. You know how rules are. Even if you don't make 'em, you still gotta live by 'em. Now," she pulled Cassandra away from her neck and looked her in the eyes. "You best be good for the new ma and pa ya gonna get. They may not understand ya like me and Big Tony, but you know how to be good for 'em. You best make me and Big Tony proud, ya hear me?"

Cassandra nodded to the older woman. "I won't make 'em hate me. I promise." She paused for a moment. "But if Big Tony gets himself a new job, and you get a house again, can you come get me? Nobody's ever gonna be as good a ma and pa as you and Big Tony."

"Yeah, I reckon' we can try to get ya when Tony gets a new job. Maybe we even try to 'dopt ya," she said with a thoughtful look in her eye.

"Really?" Cassandra said with wide eyes. "You'd really 'dopt me?"

"I don't know if the gov'ment would let us since we're so old, but I think we'll try. Now, don't get your panties all in a bunch if it takes a while. Ya know how these things are. They take time."

"So, you just remember to be on your best behavior, little missy. Don't make them ma's and pa's have to whoop ya. Ya know they aren't 'sposed to, but there's a damn sight lot of 'em that'll do it."

"I promise, I won't make 'em whoop me none, Miss Faith. I'm gonna be the best little girl they ever seen."

"That's good." She sniffled as another tear rolled down her cheek. "I love you, little one," Miss Faith said softly. "I'm gonna miss ya more than ya know. I sure do hate that I'm gonna have to let some other folks raise ya for a time."

"It's okay, Miss Faith. They're just gonna babysit me. Ain't no big deal to have someone babysit for ya."

"You're too smart for your own good sometimes, little miss. And I sure am gonna miss it." Miss Faith pulled her in for a big hug, not caring that her shoulder would hurt because of it.

"I'm only as smart as ya taught me, Miss Faith. And I sure am gonna miss you too."

Chapter 20

Captor,

    I lied because sadness is what people expect. How was I supposed to know that you would believe the truth? How was I supposed to believe that you wouldn't punish me purely because you believe *that I'm wrong?*

    Those are not my questions. They're rhetorical, and those don't count, as you have already set a precedent for. You have my word that I will not lie anymore. If you do not believe something that I say, then you may want to consider it for more than a moment, though. I have given you my promise, and if you know anything about me or my life as you say that you do, then you'll know that my promise means more than most people's.

    I have answered your question, but I do not understand my punishment. You locked me into the bed. You took my clothes off and made it seem as though you were going to rape me. You did everything to make me afraid of a rape, but you didn't do it.

    I can't decide whether you were trying to punish me through fear or through something else, and you decided against it half-way through. I am sure that the thoughts of what you could have done passed through your mind, but I can't decide what it was that changed.

    My thoughts are the only thing left to me, but the longer that I sit in this Cage, the more they become jumbled. I still do not understand your process, your needs, your desires for the resolution of this experiment on me. Which brings me to my question for the evening.

"What do you want from me?"

Cassandra Matheson

Chapter 21

The man looked at the screen, the camera moved slowly as he watched Cassandra in her sun dress playing with the kitten. *Tigger* was what she'd named it. He didn't understand the naming of an animal when there was only the one. He'd never understood the love that a person could have for an animal for that matter.

That was the problem with him, though. He didn't understand so many things. He was broken. So terribly broken. And he'd always been like that. At least for as long as he could remember.

It was time for him to pick up the food and notebook.

He walked away from the cameras, the soles of his dress shoes squeaking slightly as he walked across the hardwood floor. Dark wood beams framed the doorways of the place he called home. The drywall had a spackled look to it, and the ceilings were high.

He walked into the kitchen and poured a glass of water for himself from a filtered pitcher in the refrigerator. He looked into the mirror above the kitchen sink and rubbed the small scratch across his cheek that the kitten had given him when he'd been a fool enough to put the creature up to his face.

It wouldn't scar. Not like the cut across his eyebrow that he'd received when he was just a boy. The scar ran across his left eyebrow, splitting the line of hair in two.

He took a sip of the water and looked at himself, the sandy blond hair and green eyes that stared back at him. He was a monster logically. He knew that, but he didn't understand why the things that he did were so inherently bad. He was the man that women locked their doors against at night, but he didn't know why other men and other women weren't just like him.

When people thought of him after he was eventually caught, they wouldn't think of his past. They wouldn't think of the kindnesses he'd tried to do. All they would see would be the trail of blood that he'd left behind.

It wasn't that he was confused on what was considered right and wrong. He was fully aware of what society called right. It was the why behind it that bothered him. Society would call him a monster for killing Cassandra's boyfriend, but he was doing it to protect her from a man who didn't treat her well.

If a dog bit your child, you might forgive it after it was punished, but if it bit her again, you would have the dog put down because the danger of it doing more than a little bite was too much. It was too dangerous. And a man was so much more dangerous than a dog. All he'd done was put down a pet because it no longer followed the rules.

He set the glass down on the counter. The crystal clinked softly against the marble. Clean sounds. Sounds that reminded him that he controlled this place. He was the master of this home.

Still, after all these years, he had to remind himself that no one else controlled his life. No one would force him to do anything.

He smiled as he walked to his study. He'd built this house to have a storm shelter under it. At least that's what he'd told the architect and the building crew. After they were done, he'd done the rest of the work himself.

A steel reinforced doorframe and door were the first things he installed. The second was a circuit breaker at the bottom of the stairs. A single switch to kill all the power to the Cage.

The third, and most important part was the door at the top of the stairs. From the front, it looked like a wall. It wouldn't take a lot of looking to tell that there was a door, but at first glance, it certainly looked like a wall, and that's all that it was meant to do.

On the inside, it looked the same. If you were to walk up the stairs, it would be difficult to tell that it was a door. In order to open the door, all you had to do was push a button on the side, but in the darkness, it would be impossible find it unless you knew where it was.

The man slid the door open. It didn't make a sound. Not a squeaking. Not a groaning. Nothing. Silence. He walked inside the doorway and pushed the button on the wall, and it closed behind him, silent once again. He stepped down the stairs to his ready station.

He slid his shoes off and put on the infrared goggles. He took a deep breath as he did each time that he flipped the switch above the counter of his ready station.

Instantly, the hallway was plunged into pure darkness. No light. He knew this place. Knew every inch of the space. He pushed the button to start the infrared vision. Nothing changed. The heat in this space was always exactly the same, but that didn't matter to him. The darkness was not a place of fear for him.

He walked forward to the door and unlocked it silently. The room he was walking into was filled with darkness as well. He glanced at the space where the bed was and saw Cassandra through the goggles. She was silent and still. He knew that she was looking in his direction. He'd watched the videos of her reaction to the darkness before.

His cameras were fitted with infrared vision as well, and so he could see what happened while he was in the room. He ignored Cassandra for the moment and picked up the tray of food and the notebook.

He looked at her again, only seeing a picture of her heat, but knowing that only a foot away, she sat powerless. He had to remind himself that she was here for a reason, and it didn't matter what he wanted to do to her, he needed her.

He stepped through the door again and closed it behind him. Then he locked it. He did all of this by touch and memory. The goggles did not tell him where anything was. He brought the tray through the darkness and set it on the counter of his ready station. Then he turned off the goggles and turned on the power to the room and the hallway.

He brought the tray up to the kitchen to wash the dishes. As always, he washed the dishes before turning to the one thing that truly interested him in the world currently. The notebook.

He flipped open the page and read Cassandra's response to his question. *"How did finding your boyfriend's body in your dining room make you feel?"* How could she write this? He'd watched her, had put cameras in her home and her car. While she was walking into her house to find Craig, he'd installed a camera in her car.

She had been angry. He'd seen that in the camera. He'd watched her as she'd called the police, and he'd heard as she'd pulled over outside of the city and just screamed in anger. Not once, not even a single time, did he ever see her cry. The anger in her letter had been expected, and the anger that she'd shown because of Craig's murder had been just as expected.

The lie was unexpected. And unacceptable.

Why had she lied? He sat back and thought. Truth was the most important rule. If she couldn't be trusted to tell the truth, how could he ever learn from her? How could he find a way to love someone if he could never even understand the simpler and more dramatic emotions?

He sighed in frustration. He stood up and went to the garage for rope. It was time to teach her that he was serious.

Chapter 22

Her hair was beautiful. Most people wouldn't have understood that. People would call it a mousy brown, drab in color, and relatively unnoticeable, but he found it utterly entrancing.

When she lay in the bed, the kitten liked to pounce on the hair that gently moved on the pillow next to her. They would play like this for hours, and the man could watch them the entire time.

This playfulness had helped him to notice an anomaly, a unique difference between what he'd known about her and what he was noticing now.

He'd watched her for years, but for the first time in as long as he could remember, she was smiling without anyone around. Even in the Cage, when she played with the kitten, she smiled.

He had watched her for a very long time, and he'd noticed that she never smiled when she was alone. She smiled regularly around other people, but it was as though she were a different person around them. The mask that she wore was flawless. It was likely that not even she had realized that she never smiled when she was alone.

But she smiled because of the kitten. It was a real smile, an unneeded and completely natural smile. And the man didn't understand it at all.

He shook his head. Now was not the time to wonder about things like that.

Now was the time for her punishment.

He walked into the study again carrying several lengths of rope and a capped hypodermic needle. Through the hidden doorway, he moved down the stairs. He slipped off his shoes and sat the rope on the counter. He didn't need that quite yet.

He put on the goggles and took a deep breath before flipping the switch and plunging the world into darkness. He moved quickly, knowing that she would be surprised by the unusual extra darkness this morning.

He opened the door and walked into the room. She was still on the bed, and the kitten was nowhere to be seen. He stepped towards Cassandra rather than the desk as he normally did. For the first time since her capture, she heard a clear sound in the darkness, the sharp click of the man unsnapping the cap of the hypodermic needle.

Her breath caught in her throat as he plunged the needle into her shoulder. She tried to get away, never making a sound, but he held her still with the other hand. He pushed the fluid into her body, and he felt her slump under him. He would give the drugs time to kick in before he turned on the light and began to work.

He felt her body, felt her skin under his hand, and he shivered. He'd never felt like this before as he touched someone. He'd watched Cassandra for years as he tried to understand human emotions, but he'd only touched her once before: when he'd knocked her unconscious the first time.

He hadn't known her then. Not like he knew her now. He'd watched her. He'd seen her react to other people. That was different than this, though. Now, she was focused on him, and that changed everything.

He ran his hand over her skin in the darkness, and even without seeing her, he knew that he wanted more than to just talk to her. He'd fucked other women. How would he have ever expected to understand love if he hadn't "made love" to a woman before. It hadn't worked.

For the first time, he felt different. A surge of something irrational ran through the man, and he found himself wondering if he was doing the right thing.

He stepped back and nearly tripped over the chair as he moved away from the bed, his purpose suddenly clouded. He heard the hiss before he turned around, and then he felt the kitten as it leaped off the desk and onto his shirt. Tiny little claws dug into the fabric that clung to his body as the kitten climbed the man as though he were a tree.

The man reached behind him, trying to get to the little ball of orange and white, but it was hanging onto the middle of his back, and he couldn't reach it. Slowly, the kitten climbed up his back and found the exposed skin of his neck. He bit down hard on the skin and tore at his flesh, making the man curse.

But the kitten was high enough on the man's back that he could reach the creature, and he pulled him away. The man panted as he held the kitten tightly as it tried to claw and bite at the hand that held him. The tiny claws and teeth may not have been enough to seriously wound or kill a man, but they were certainly enough to be painful.

The man walked around the room without needing the light. He found the cage that the kitten had been brought to Cassandra in, and he put it back in. Closing it quickly, the kitten continued to hiss and attack the metal of the cage, but he was now harmless to the man.

The man reached around to the back of his neck and felt the wetness. Blood. The little creature had done its damnedest to kill the man, and for the first time, the man smiled as he thought of the creature.

Cats were not known to be protective, but the tiny little ball of fluff had believed itself strong enough to protect Cassandra against a large predator such as himself. Or at least, it had believed that it was worth it to defend the woman.

He walked back to hallway, and he flipped the switch turning on the lights again. The shirt he wore would be ruined from the blood stain. It wouldn't be the first time he'd have to burn a shirt because of a blood stain, but it would be the first that he'd do so from *his* blood rather than the blood of his victim.

He gathered up the coils of rope and brought them into the Cage. He ran his hands under Cassandra's body to lift her up, his previous irrationality now gone once more. He pulled the dress up over her head being careful not to pull her arms at any angles that would cause her injury. Quickly, he undid her bra and panties, leaving her completely naked on the twin bed with white sheets.

He'd put her in this bed completely naked only five days before, but it seemed different now. He felt something strange when he thought of the woman who lay unconscious below him.

He hadn't wanted to touch her then. Hadn't wanted to run his fingers over her slightly tanned skin. For a moment, he was tempted to see if making love with Cassandra would be different than the women he'd fucked before. The thought was gone as soon as it appeared in his mind, though. He would not break her any more than he had to.

Fear would be more than enough of a punishment.

He began to bind her leg, careful not to cut off the flow of blood. Neither of them would be able to see if there was any kind of a color change. She wouldn't know that it was not his purpose to injure her. He had to be extremely careful with his knotwork.

He spread her legs, exposing her to the open air, and for the very first time since this experiment had begun, he felt lust begin to stir inside of him. He felt the blood begin to rush to it, and he stepped back once again to look at the woman passed out on the bed before him.

She was spread open invitingly, but that wasn't what had made him slow his work. It was the split-second image of her bound like this, but with her eyes open watching him. The combination of fear and desire in the fleeting fantasy had been the first thing to make him desire her since he'd begun watching her all those years ago.

He shook his head. He had a purpose, a reason behind this experiment. It was more difficult than he'd expected to be around her now, but it was not impossible. He'd done challenging things many times in his life, and this was nowhere near the most difficult.

He finished tying her body, and he left her in the room, waiting for her to wake up to begin her punishment.

Chapter 23

Cassandra,

You ask me what I want from you, and once upon a time, I would have said that I wanted to understand your motivation and your ability to continue on even when hurt over and over again. I would like to tell you that this is still true, but things have changed, and I don't know what it is that I want.

One thing is true still. I want to know you. I want you to continue to tell me truths. Something is changing inside of me that I had never expected, and I cannot stop it now. I apologize for the inconvenience to you, but I have spent my life trying to find a way to become whole, to find the soul that people have told me that I am lacking.

This is the closest I have ever been to finding anything like that. I think. I could be wrong, and this could all be a waste. I would say that I am sorry to have done this to you if that is true, but that would be a lie. That would be what people expected out of me. I was taught to "say sorry", just as all children are, but I refuse to tell you lies, and that is exactly what it would be.

What is it that I want? I guess what I want is to feel more than I felt yesterday. I want more than a glimmer of humanity. I didn't feel anything when I was surrounded by destruction, but maybe when I am surrounded by goodness, at least part of it will touch me. Maybe.

This should all be clearer and simpler. It was once upon a time. It seems that emotions, regardless of what they are, tend to muddy the *water of purpose. Although these emotions have been my lifelong goal, there are times that I am very glad to have never had them cloud my purpose before.*

This brings me to my question. I repeat, "What emotions did you feel when you saw Craig's body?"

Chapter 24

The man watched Cassandra Matheson as he always did. 3 am and the bars were closed. She'd stayed until they'd kicked her out again. Slurring and stumbling, she was barely conscious.

The watcher followed her silently, his body hidden in shadows. He knew that the subtlety was unnecessary. She barely knew how to get home much less that someone was following her.

She hadn't always been like this. When she'd first gotten to college, she'd stayed safe. She'd made good decisions. Yes, she'd gone to parties, but she'd always surrounded herself with friends and she never put herself in risky situations.

Tonight, she was not being safe. She had a mile of unlit alleys and side streets to walk down before she made it home. The watcher did not hide from Cassandra. He hid from the ones that walked in shadows and hunted the innocent and the weak.

He knew that he would have prey tonight. The woman he followed was too good of bait. Her beauty made them want her, and her drunkenness made it easy. She wore tight fitting clothes that showed plenty of skin.

The watcher saw the glint of steel in the moonlight as a man stepped into the alley behind Cassandra, and he smiled. This creature that hunted the woman he watched thought he was at home in the darkness. He thought that the silence and the night kept him safe, but the watcher had lived in the dark for his entire life, and this man was just a visitor.

He was a thin man, and he wore simple clothes. Dark jeans and a dark shirt. They did not hide him from the watcher. His shoes made noise on the concrete of the alleyway. The blue and white sneakers were like shining beacons in the night, loud and bright.

The watcher wore simple clothes as well. A red button-up dress shirt and black slacks to go with his dress shoes. When he walked out of the alley, no one would expect he was a predator. No one would step to the other side of the street as he passed them.

A true predator did not make his prey want to hide. He blended into any environment, not just the shadows of a deserted alley.

Moving silently, the watcher came from behind the man. Men who preyed on women in dark alleys were strange creatures. They felt strong, like they were predators, and yet every motion was wrong.

This man held the knife wrong. Too loose of a grip. It was turned just slightly so that he would have to correct during any swing. It wasn't even a good knife for the job. The knife did not have a hilt to protect his hand when stabbing, and so it would only be good to slice with lest he injure himself.

The watcher chided the man silently in his mind as he did with most of his prey. That was the problem when you only hunted soft and sweet creatures. That was the problem when you never had to become stronger, faster, or smarter. That was the problem with humans in general. They never extended themselves unless it was necessary.

It was good that the watcher had been born without any humanity.

So when the watcher reached out to grip his prey's weapon, he was calm and free of any nervousness. This was a motion he had practiced enough times on other prey, other weak predators. His motion was quick, silent, and effective. When he came away with the knife before the man realized what had happened, only his prey gasped in surprise. A soft whisper in the darkness. He turned to see the watcher, his eyes wide.

Predators never expect to be hunted.

When the blade flashed silver in the moonlight, the man tried to gasp again. This time, it was a gurgle as crimson flowed from the gash across his neck. The watcher quickly glanced at the woman he was following. She hadn't heard anything. That made things simpler.

The blade flashed again and again, quick stabs in the darkness. Once for each lung. The watcher did not have time to deal with the man who had once thought himself a predator.

He had not sought the man out. He had not even brought a weapon with him, knowing that anyone who preyed on the innocent at night would be carrying their own.

It was surprising how simplistic the average man was when he decided to hunt in the night. The majority would never use a gun. That would draw too much attention if it was actually needed, and it was just more difficult to acquire one that would not lead directly back to him.

Even more surprising than their simplicity was their laziness. Was that why they became predators? Because they were too lazy to do things the typical way? Was this man who had been willing to hurt an innocent woman simply too lazy to get a job or too lazy to convince a woman to get into bed with him?

He looked down at the man who was still leaking blood from the cut in his throat. Only seconds had passed, and he reached up to the watcher. The man would only be conscious for a moment or two more with how quickly he was bleeding out.

The watcher smiled down at him. Laziness and simplicity had been this man's death sentence, and the watcher was all too happy to have been the executioner.

The watcher was a monster. He knew that. He roamed the dark, no different than the man at his feet. The difference between them was that while this dying man had been a human playing in the dark, the watcher was something foreign. A soulless monster who hunted every night.

The watcher pulled the man behind a dumpster. He was still trying to breathe, still trying to stand up, to escape. It wouldn't happen. He would be unconscious in the next minute and dead in the next five.

All of this was because a simple man had decided to pretend to be a monster. Why did no one tell these people to leave the darkness to the real monsters, to the ones who did not belong in the light?

With a single look down at the trail of blood, he turned back to the woman who he watched. Tonight, he would continue his watch, but tomorrow, he would need to find another woman, another experiment.

The woman that he currently had in a cage was barely more than an animal and needed to be disposed of. It was too bad. He had thought that a beautiful woman might have been the key. She *had been* beautiful with long mousy brown hair to begin with, but after a month in the cage, she disgusted him.

Eventually, he would find a way to fix himself. Then he would be able to leave the shadows and understand the ones that walk in the light.

Chapter 25

Captor,

It is good that you have begun to feel something. I would say that it makes me happy, but that would be a lie. In fact, if we are both being truthful, the only reason that I care whether you still breathe is because you hold the key to my cage. That may or may not make me a horrible person, and thus you may be unable to surround yourself with the goodness you so desperately wish for.

Regardless of my feelings for you, I am bound to you until you release me, and so I will comply with your needs. You want to know what I felt? I felt anger. Pure and unadulterated hatred. Towards you. You took a piece of my life and destroyed it. Craig was not the best boyfriend. I knew this.

His cheating did not matter to me. Not then, and not now. It was unsightly, and if he had been unable to keep his hands off my friend, I would have been forced to break up with him, but I am not a jealous woman. I never have been. I certainly never wished him dead for it.

It doesn't matter if he was the worst man on the planet. It was not your place to decide his fate. It was not your place to determine whether he lived or died, but more than that, it was not your place to even decide whether we continued to date or not. If you had been so worried about my delicate emotions, then you should have simply brought the issue to my attention.

You seem to understand my life, so I will assume that you know of my past. I have been put through so many things that a little cheating was not something that would hurt me. On the other hand, knowing that a madman had killed my boyfriend and then have him kidnap me and keep me in his basement would still be pretty high up on my list of fucked up situations.

How is it that you can both hold me up on a pedestal and ignore the fact that you have taken away my freedom?

Cassandra Matheson

Chapter 26

1 year before the Cage, Age 30

"You can't take our children!" the woman screamed. She wore tight fitting Western style jeans and a plaid shirt that was cut in a form fitting way to accentuate her large breasts. Black hair that had been straightened streamed down to the middle of her back.

She'd been born in privilege. Her husband had been born in privilege. And yet her children were in danger. She had a better chance than most to give her children a life that they would look back on with fondness. Instead, she and her husband had brought them only pain and suffering.

Cassandra looked at the woman who was being held back by her husband and smiled. She'd never been good at calming down these types of situations. That was something that she was supposed to learn. It was the one part of her job that she was repeatedly chastised about, and she didn't care one bit.

The police officers escorted the children into Cassandra's car, a simple silver sedan. Perfectly clean, but not expensive. "Nicki, I'm not taking your children. I'm saving your children. From you. You have hurt them too many times, and it's time that someone helped them."

The woman lunged at Cassandra, but her husband did his best to hold her back. She broke free of his grasp, and as she took the last step to Cassandra, instead of panic like she expected, she saw pure glee on Cassandra's face.

Nicki reached out to Cassandra as she ran at her, and Cassandra simply sidestepped the woman's charge. She left her leg out and brought her hand down harshly on the woman's back, tripping the woman in the middle of her charge. Her momentum forced her to the ground fast enough that she didn't have time to catch her fall.

When she rolled onto her back to look at Cassandra again, a police officer had already stepped in front of her. Blood ran down cheek and nose where she'd scraped her face against the pavement. The seeping blood mixed with tears born of anger.

And Cassandra couldn't stop smiling as Nicki glared at her from the ground. This woman deserved to be bleeding. She deserved to hurt. Cassandra's only regret was that she had no way to make the woman hurt worse. That she couldn't force the same trauma and misery on the woman that she had inflicted on her daughter.

The little girl, Emily, was seven. She had been five when Nicki's brother, Jared, had begun molesting her. Nicki's brother had already been arrested, but Cassandra had pushed to have the kids taken from Nicki and her husband's home because Nicki had done nothing to stop the abuse.

She'd known about it. Emily had told Cassandra about the time that she'd told her mom about how Uncle Jared had touched her and how it had hurt. Nicki's husband had lost his job and Jared was living with them to help with the bills.

He'd been a transient truck driver, living out of motel rooms when not on the road, but when Nicki had asked for help, he'd come. And he'd used Emily in payment. Nicki denied knowing about it. Her husband did too.

Emily didn't lie, though. She said that Jared had hurt her. That he hadn't just touched her, that he'd made her bleed. Emily had been crying when she relived those memories for Cassandra. She'd cried and cried, and when Cassandra had asked her if her mom would keep her safe, Emily had said that no one would keep her safe. Not even Mommy.

That's when Cassandra had decided to ruin them. She hadn't simply taken their children. She'd done it at Nicki's family reunion. Jared had been arrested immediately to protect Emily, but Cassandra had waited three days to take the children out of the home.

She'd had to call in a lot of favors, but doing it in the middle of the circle of 'family and friends' that watched as Nicki lost her children was worth the cost.

"Your brother molested and raped your only daughter, Nicki. And you protected him. You worried more about the rent payment than about the fact that a grown man was having his way with your five year old daughter. You're a monster, and if I have it my way, you'll never see your children again."

"You should have done anything else. I would be more compassionate towards you if you'd robbed people, whored yourself out, or lived on the street. Anything would have been better than giving your daughter to a monster. Anything."

Cassandra walked away from the woman who lay on the ground. Everyone that Nicki cared about knew what had happened now. Cassandra couldn't prosecute Nicki. She hadn't been the one to hurt Emily, and it would be impossible to prove that she'd known about it. Cassandra only had the word of a seven year old. That would never hold up in court, but her family and friends would stop supporting her.

Everyone she had cared about would abandon her. Her crimes would not go unpunished even if the law could do nothing to bring justice to the woman, the people that had been closest to her would provide the punishment that she needed.

And Jared would be forced to endure his own abuse in prison. She would make sure of that. Cassandra was not a child anymore, and the monsters of the world did not scare her.

Not anymore.

She climbed into her silver sedan and smiled at the children in her back seat. "How would you like to get some ice cream and chat?" she asked them.

Chapter 27

19 days Since the Cage, Age 31

Tigger pounced on the cotton mouse that he'd had when Cassandra had received him as her first reward. She'd gotten more rewards as the days and nights had passed. Her favorite books sat on the desk and her favorite music was programmed into an iPod.

She had received a cake at one point and eaten it over three days. She had new clothes, and her latest gift had been a vibrator.

She had not used it.

That didn't change the fact that at least a part of her wanted to masturbate just from boredom. The entertainment options were growing with each truthful answer she gave, but they were all the same. Mental escapes. She hadn't lied since her punishment. That was the rule. No lying.

That didn't mean that she hadn't started planning her escape though. She stood at one end of the room. She closed her eyes and walked slowly across the room, stopping in front of her chair without touching it and then taking one step to the side. She took two steps forward and then one to the side. If she'd done it right, she wouldn't feel the chair at all.

Instead, she bumped into it on her sideways step back into the line she'd been walking. She sighed and looked at the chair. She went back to the corner and closed her eyes again. She had to learn to judge distance like this in a single snapshot in her mind so that she could walk around the room with her eyes closed.

She would never be able to walk through the world without her eyesight, but that didn't mean that she shouldn't be able to walk around her tiny Cage with her eyes closed. She started the exercise again, and when she tried to move around the chair, she managed to slide past it.

She opened her eyes triumphantly, and she began the process all over again. There was nothing she could do except keep practicing. She was getting better. Initially, it had taken her hours before she'd managed to guess the number of steps correctly. Now it was simply two to three tries.

She was getting better, but if she were trying to escape the Cage, she was going to have to be able to move quickly enough in the blackness to overpower the Monster. That would mean that she'd have to use the chair on him.

She would only get one chance. One single swing with the chair was all she'd get. If she missed, she was sure that her captor could catch her, and she'd be punished even if it wasn't in the rules. But if she could beat him to death with the chair, she would be able to find her way out of the blackness eventually. Even if it took days.

If she could kill him, then there would be time for her to slowly puzzle out how to turn the lights on and then manage to escape. No one else knew she was here. Cassandra couldn't believe anything else as that would mean that there was no way to escape. If there was even one other person to rescue the man she attacked, she would be caught without a doubt. She could come up with no other plans, and so she just had to trust.

Before she could do any of that, she had to learn to move in the nothingness. And that was far easier said than done. Her footsteps were slow, and yet she still stumbled on everything. She needed to be able to run with the lights off. She needed to be able to track the almost impossible sound of the man's footsteps enough that she could hit him with a chair.

And so she continued with her practice. She had time. That was all she had anymore.

Chapter 28

Cassandra,

You're right about my hypocritical behavior. I have tried to act in your favor for as long as I can remember, and until I "locked you in a cage", I do not believe that I ever worked against that desire. My answer is that I had no other choice.

My lifelong path has been one of learning about myself and about everyone else. People everywhere have emotions towards each other. They care about their parents' health. They care about the poor man on the street asking for change. They care about all types of things.

I don't. I don't care that Craig died. I did it, and I walked away from the scene without any emotion towards the act. I was not joyous, and I was not sad. Craig needed to die, and I was the only one who could do it for you.

I didn't feel bad that you wouldn't have someone to hold you at night. I didn't feel bad that you would have to sleep elsewhere while the police unsuccessfully investigated the scene. I didn't even feel bad that you would be afraid.

My parents died a long time ago. I was young then, only six years old, and I didn't cry. I wasn't sad. All I felt was annoyance that I would have to leave the woods that I'd hunted in.

I am broken, Cassandra. Absolutely, and completely broken. My goal is to fix the broken pieces no matter the cost. I would prefer it *if the cost were someone other than you, but I don't believe that is possible. I've tried, and those experiments were failures.*

I truly hope that this does not turn into a failure, but that is part of the reason that I am keeping my identity hidden from you. If I were to show you who I was, I would be forced to kill you after the experiment was over.

I have done everything I can to keep you safe and keep you sane within the bounds of the experiment. If anything, you are the one person in the world that I 'care' about, although it is more an admiration of your strength than an emotion.

Now it is time for my question. "Why do you care? Why do you care about everyone?"

Chapter 29

Cassandra stood in the shower, and she closed her eyes. With a deep breath, she pictured the Cage in all of the complexity that she'd left it in. The chair was in front of the bathroom door. The nightstand had been moved in front of her bed.

She counted her steps as she rushed through the room. Her body knew the path. It had memorized the steps to the bathroom door. She trusted her feet to know where to move, when to shift. Reaching out a hand to touch the doorframe, she verified her position on the mental map that she'd made in her mind.

Without slowing down or opening her eyes, she pulled at the frame and turned towards the door. Her toes gripped the carpet under her as she shifted her weight.

She had tried to keep track of her steps with counts, but that never worked when she moved quickly or changed step size.

It had taken almost a week of consistent work to realize that there was no way that she'd be able to keep track of her position with a step count. She'd accepted the difficult truth that the only way that she would be able to move in the darkness was if it became instinctual.

She'd closed her eyes two weeks ago, and until today, she'd kept them closed nearly the entire time. Today was her test.

She reached out her hand as she approached the chair, and just as her fingers touched the wood, she leapt to the side, her foot barely touching the baseboard on her left. She leapt again, this time at an angle. Always towards the door, she never stopped moving.

Two more large steps, and without verifying her position, she jumped to the side, hoping to land on her bed. Instead, her foot caught the blanket, and she tumbled onto the floor. It was not the first time that she'd made the mistake of forgetting the blanket during her movements.

In an instant, Tigger jumped through the air from his perch on the nightstand and landed on Cassandra's chest. She opened her eyes and began laughing at him as he growled and clawed at the air. "Fearsome beast!" she said as she reached out and snagged him off her chest.

He immediately began to try to escape Cassandra's grasp. His tail swished in the air as he yowled loudly, his way of yelling at Cassandra for being so terrible. She ignored his pleas for freedom as she held him tightly to her chest.

Finally, she let him go and stood up to look at what had caused her fall. She'd worked hard to make this route instinctual. Everything had been working out well until she'd hit that blanket. She needed to remember to make her bed every day. It would be easier to do that than to remember what it looked like from memory.

These were the little details that made all the difference in Cassandra's training. She looked at Tigger as he jumped around the blanket on the bed. He made little rushing noises as he zipped across it.

Once again, Cassandra thought about how hard she'd worked at trying to pinpoint the kitten while she was practicing. She could hear him on the furniture sometimes. Sometimes. Most of the time, he was silent. On the bed, she could feel him when she was on the bed, and she could hear him sometimes when he ran. When he was sneaking, he was silent though.

The most impossible place to find him was on the carpet. The little ball of fur was just too tiny to make any sound on the carpet. It didn't matter if he was running or if he was sneaking. If he was on the floor, there was no way of finding him. Cassandra had finally learned to simply accept it as a fact.

She smiled at him, and he ran up to the edge of the bed. He gave her his bird face where he cocked his head to the side in confusion, and then he turned around erratically and raced off.

Cassandra just shook her head at him and closed her eyes for another bit of practice. The faster she learned to move without sight, the faster she'd be able to escape.

Chapter 30

Captor,

    You asked me why I still care again. I only have the simplest of answers for you. Because that is what you're supposed to do.

    You say that you're broken, but we're all broken. Everyone is broken in some way.

    I'm broken. You have to know that. I went back to work two days after you killed Craig. They told me to stay home, but I didn't know what else to do. So I went to work anyways. At least while I was there, I could do some good for someone.

    The world is a horrible place, my dear Captor. You act as though you got dealt a bad hand, but think about what would have happened if you'd been forced to feel all of the terrible in the world. Think about what would have happened if you'd been forced to feel the pain of your parents dying.

    Why would you look for emotions in a world that strives to only bring you pain? I wouldn't look for them if I were you. There's nothing but pain. Sure, there may be some moments of love, but the love is always stripped away.

    My parents died when I was four. I watched them die. I still remember their faces looking through their upstairs window at me. They saw me, and then they died. Crushed to death in a fire.

    They were good people. They loved me. They hugged and kissed me every night. My mother read me stories before bed. They bought me nice clothes and cooked good food. They were the people that you read about.

And then they died.

Yes, I felt good things when I was with them, but then all the good was taken from me. They are glorious memories from my four-year-old mind. More than any of the good memories, I remember that scene in the fire.

Ash on my cheeks being held by a neighbor with a name I still don't remember. I was wearing a pair of pink pajamas with a fox on the front. My mother always dressed me in pink. I saw them, my mother and father, struggling with their window, and I was happy because they always made me happy when they were there.

Except this time, they died. I stared at them as the flaming roof fell onto them and killed the most wonderful part of my memory. If I hadn't been able to feel anything, I wouldn't have been forced to feel the most awful feelings in the world. I wouldn't have been hurting so badly that I tried to burn down my first foster home.

Captor, you are far better off never feeling. Trust me.

Here is my question to you, "What do I have to do to leave?"

Cassandra Matheson

Chapter 31

"Are you stupid?" The woman's face bunched up around her lips as she squinted at Cassandra.

"No ma'am. I ain't stupid. Why you always callin' me that?" Cassandra asked her as politely as she knew how. She'd promised that she'd be good for her next ma and pa.

"You talk like you're from some redneck trailer park, but your file says that your dad was a banker and your mom was a teacher. How is it that you don't know how to speak correctly?" The woman, Francesca, wore a yellow and blue dress that was tied at the waist. Her ample bust threatened to spill out as she bent over slightly.

She was a pretty woman who did what she could to accentuate her beauty. Her bleach blond hair was shoulder length and she wore it in a ponytail. Thick lips that were always coated in red lipstick had a tendency to glare at the children instead of smile.

"I talk like my old ma, Miss Faith, talked. She was the nicest woman I ever met, 'cept my real ma, of course." Cassandra held her hands behind her back and didn't look Francesca in the eye.

"You'll need to learn to speak correctly, little girl. I won't tolerate an idiot." She sat a long oval table that would be able to seat all of the foster children that Francesca and her husband George had collected.

"Yes ma'am. I'll do my best, Miss Franny." Cassandra kept looking down, worried that if she looked up, she'd struggle to keep from laughing at Miss Franny as she put on her snarly face.

"Go on, little girl. Get back to your chores. Your sisters and brothers will show you what you need to do." She lit a cigarette and looked at the wall across from her.

Cassandra walked slowly through the house. Running in the house was not allowed. Miss Franny had told her that as soon as she'd been placed with them. She passed the door under the stairs that never opened. The space under the door showed that there was nothing but darkness inside that room.

Susan had crept up next to Cassandra as Cassandra walked towards where everyone was working. Susan was two years older than Cassandra and had bright red hair and a lot of freckles. She wasn't trying to sneak up on Cassandra, but after living with Miss Franny and Mr. George for two years, she'd learned to make almost no noise when she walked. *Silence was safety.*

"What did they tell you?" she whispered to Cassandra as they both picked up wet rags. Today was window day. Paul and Joe, the two boys, would climb onto the roof and hold each other's legs as they hung down and got the top windows that no one could reach outside, and Susan and Cassandra would stack furniture on the inside to get the highest points on the inside of the house.

"She called me an idiot cause of the way I talk," she whispered back. "I'm gonna get whooped if I don't start talkin' right. She didn't say it like that, but that's what she meant."

"Cassandra, that means you have to learn to talk right. Getting a spanking isn't what you need to be scared of." She looked around as though Miss Franny or Mr. George might overhear. "They'll do a lot worse than spank you, Cassandra."

"Like what? What's worse than a whoo... I mean a spanking?" Cassandra asked. Susan started washing the bottom windows and Cassandra followed her.

"You never know what they'll do. If you get a spanking, it could be so bad that you can't sit down for a week cause your butt's all bruised up so bad. But... it could be worse than that. Just don't make them punish you Cassandra. It's always bad when someone gets punished."

Susan shivered even in the summer heat. They began scrubbing the windows being careful not to touch the paint that peeled up from the window frames. Susan said that one boy who'd been careless had been forced to scrape all the paint off all the window frames and then to repaint them all before he got any more food. It took him three days.

They moved as swiftly as they could. Susan wore a simple dress that was all light purple with no decoration. Cassandra had been given a dress in a similar style but was a faded brown. Both of the dresses had been worn by other girls, and there were numerous patches on both of them.

As they were finishing up, Cassandra laughed loudly at something that Susan whispered to her, and Miss Franny stomped into the room.

"What's going on in here?" she demanded.

"Nothing, Miss Franny. We were just finishing the windows like we're supposed to. See. We've only got this one left." She gave the older woman a big smile.

Miss Franny walked up to the windows that they'd started with and she ran her finger along the edge. She pulled her finger back and there were several grains of sand on them. "Do you call this clean?" she asked accusingly.

"I'm sorry Miss Franny. We'll redo them right now. We didn't mean to miss any of the dirt." She picked up the bucket of water and brought it back to the beginning of the line as Miss Franny watched.

Cassandra followed Susan, trying to be as quiet as she could just like Susan, but she tripped over a board that stuck out of the floor just barely. She fell on the floor and hit the bucket that Susan had just set down, knocking it over and spraying water all over.

"What is wrong with you, idiot girl?" Miss Franny shrieked. Susan immediately righted the bucket and ran to get a towel to mop up the water. Cassandra stood up slowly, and Miss Franny moved in front of her to begin screaming at her.

"I knew that you were an idiot, but are you telling me that you can't even manage to walk without falling down and knocking things over?"

"No ma'am. I can walk fine," Cassandra said softly. Susan got back into the room as Miss Franny said, "Then why in God's name did you knock over the bucket?"

"Miss Franny, it was just an accident," Susan said softly coming to Cassandra's aid. "I'm going to clean it up and it'll be like it never happened." Miss Franny turned her frustration on Susan.

"I think you're getting mighty big for your britches little girl." Susan began to back up slowly, no different than a scared dog backing up from an angry master.

"I think that if you're going to come to little Cassandra's rescue, then maybe it's you that should be punished instead of her. Maybe that'll teach you both a lesson." She reached out and grabbed Susan by the back of the neck and began to drag her into the dining room where she'd first talked to Cassandra.

"Go get the rest of the children, idiot girl. Doesn't do any good to punish a child unless everyone watches." Cassandra ran outside and told the boys what had happened. They walked with solidarity into the dining room. All four children stood at the doorway as George walked into the room from the other side.

George was a mid-sized man who'd begun balding early in life and had just stopped losing his hair, leaving the greying hair in large thin patches. He cut it himself to save money, so it ended up being all different lengths.

He had strong sinewy arms and legs with wrinkled skin from the years in the sun as a farmer. Everything on him was lean from his pock-marked face to his neck all the way down to the feet that were tucked away in worn brown leather boots. All of it except for the round beer belly that he would rub and scratch unceremoniously when he was thinking.

More than likely, he wouldn't have been a horrible man, not like Miss Franny, but he would rather burn the house and all the children in it to the ground before he'd upset his wife.

"George, this girl needs a spanking. She smarted off to me." He raised his eyebrow at Susan and shrugged his shoulders.

"Alright, Franny." He undid his belt and pulled it from his belt loops.

Susan began to cry, and Miss Franny told her, "You'd better shut your mouth until you start getting hit or I'll give you extra." Susan began to sniffle, trying to keep her tears from falling.

Miss Franny pointed at Joe and said, "Joe, you get on the other side of the table and hold Susan's arms. You'd better not let her go or you'll get double what she gets."

Susan shook as she bent over the table and looked at Joe who grimaced at her as he took her wrists in his hands. "All the rest of you kids need to get on this side of her so you can watch as she's punished. Maybe it'll teach you all not to mouth off anymore. And if you look away, she'll get more too, so you'd better pay attention."

Miss Franny picked up Susan's dress, exposing her underwear, and Mr. George swung the belt in a full strike. The sound was loud enough that it shook Cassandra who watched in fear.

Susan screamed, and Mr. George swung again. Cassandra began to shake. She'd never seen anyone hurt like this. Never before had she heard of a child being hit hard enough that they had to be held down.

Susan screamed again and again as Mr. George gave her a total of eight strikes of the belt. They couldn't be called a swat as each hit had blistered skin and left bruises criss-crossing her bottom. Mr. George put his belt back on and Miss Franny let her dress down before addressing Susan who was sobbing as she lay immobile on the table.

"Now, you need to get back to cleaning those windows. I better not find a single speck of dust on them when you're done. Do you hear me, little girl?"

Susan barely got the "Yes, ma'am," out through her sobs. Miss Franny walked away towards her bedroom, and the other children rushed to help Susan up. They hushed her and held her, and Cassandra stood apart from them, still shaking.

The boy named Joe walked up to Cassandra and whispered, "You're new here, but you've got to go clean those windows or you'll be on the table next. That wasn't that bad. Susan will be fine, but if you don't get to work and be quiet about it, Miss Franny will do something real bad."

He pulled at her arm to shake her out of it, and Cassandra yanked her arm away from the boy. She pulled her lips up in a snarl, like an animal. "Don't touch me!" she whispered to the boy before turning to the room with the windows.

Chapter 32

Cassandra,

This was a wasted question. I can only let you go once you've taught me to feel. I already told you that. I wish I could let you go, but this is the last chance I have to find my humanity. If it doesn't work, then I don't know what I will do.

Let's talk about this cat of yours. He attacked me. Did you know that? When I tied you to the bed, the little furball tried to kill me by climbing the back of my shirt and biting my neck. I still have several scabs because of it.

You have done similar things, haven't you? You've fought to protect people against much more powerful people, and you could have been hurt because of it. I can't seem to understand why you always seem to ignore the danger to yourself, ignore the cost, and save or protect another person or even a creature.

I struggle to understand your motivation. Is it this elusive "love"? The Greeks would have called it Agape or unconditional love. The early Christians would have called the actions Christ-like, but then again, the early Christians were very strong believers in martyrdom as well.

This type of action has always confused me the most. I could understand it if the person owed you the favor. I could understand if you could stand to profit from it in some way, but you never do.

It's a puzzle to me, so maybe you could explain it to me. My specific question, though, is "What does love feel like?"

Chapter 33

Tigger jumped on her dress as Cassandra pulled it over her head, and she had to stop half-way through the process. "You little shit," she muttered as she grabbed the little orange and white puff ball from the bottom of the dress before pulling it over her head and putting it on the bed.

She let the kitten go as she stripped off her bra and panties and carried them to the pile of items that she'd built in the corner. She folded the dress, a deep red and white one that must have cost a fortune and put it at the top of the pile. She looked at the pile from the other side of the room as she sat down on the carpet.

Tigger stalked toward her, but instead of pouncing on her toes or trying to attack her hands as he normally would have, he curled up next to her leg and softly licked the bare skin.

"I know you can hear me," she said loudly enough that there would be no mistaking what she said.

"I've stayed silent for a month and a half. I've read your letters and I've responded. I've followed your rules, and I've done everything I could do to help you. I've been truthful." She began to pet Tigger softly, and he started purring.

"I know you won't talk to me. I know that nothing I do will help my situation. I can't imagine that anything I do would help you to learn to care about another person. I don't know how anyone could expect to learn from watching and talking to another person. It just doesn't make sense."

"I've been quiet this entire time, and I'll probably be quiet again, but I had to say it. I know you're watching me. You're always watching me. I see the cameras following me. You know what I'm doing, and I'm at the point that I don't care anymore."

Cassandra stood up and Tigger hissed at her as she picked him up. "Don't give me any more gifts. I won't use them. I want my cat, and I want the only gift left for you to give me, my freedom. Until then, none of the gifts matter."

And then the room was plunged into darkness.

Chapter 34

Captor,

You want to know what love feels like? I thought you said you knew me. I have loved only four people in my life. My biological parents and two foster parents who you almost assuredly do not know. The feeling of that love left me long ago.

How do I love? I don't. It's as simple as that. I was told once that love was the thing that held our broken pieces together. I've never found anyone who could do that for me. We're not so different in that regard.

There is no unconditional love within me. I do not love without reason or without purpose. Dear Captor, I do not understand where you came up with that idea.

If you had watched me as closely as you say you have, then you'd know that I cannot love the children that I work with. Love leaves you open to the pain of losing them. If anything, that is the lesson that I wish I could teach you. Stop trying to search for the emotions that you seem so desperate to find.

I don't understand why you won't talk instead of these letters. It has been so long since I heard a voice other than my own. If you're bound and determined to follow through with this plan of yours, then don't you think that a closer connection to me would be beneficial?

Maybe then we could accelerate this process and I can go home sooner. I have decided that I'm willing to do whatever it takes to make things move more quickly. Stop trying to ply my emotions with gifts. I won't accept them, and they'll go in the pile with the rest.

"How can I help you to learn faster so that I can leave more quickly?"

Cassandra Matheson

Chapter 35

The man paced across the viewing room. Cassandra's letter had upset him. He understood her desire to leave, but she was so focused on how his quest for humanity was a waste of time. He had been prepared for her to want out of the Cage. He'd been prepared for a lot of things but watching her naked in the Cage again was difficult. More difficult than he'd ever expected.

He brushed the blond hair from his face in his frustration. He'd let it get longer than normal as he'd spent more and more time watching his captive. Infatuation had turned into pure unadulterated obsession. He had no other thoughts beyond Cassandra these days.

His dress shoes tapped on the hard floor as he paced in the small room. What was he supposed to do? He couldn't let her go. He couldn't abandon his quest either. He wanted to make her happy, wanted to help her leave as fast as possible, but he couldn't give up on his last chance for humanity.

Maybe she was right. Maybe being able to talk to her would be enough. But could he stand to be that close to her and do nothing? That day that she'd been punished had almost been too much for him. He knew that his obsession had gotten worse since then.

Would he be able to control the desires that had begun to fill his mind? Fantasies of the flesh had filled his dreams for the last week, and they were getting stronger. He had all the power. If he gave into the desires, he would be no better than the monsters in her past.

The man sighed and walked back into the kitchen to look at himself in the mirror. He had gone years without seeing himself in a mirror as a child, and now that he could look into one any time he wanted, he took advantage of it.

He'd grown lax in his grooming and hygiene. He had been immaculate in his grooming for his entire adult life. From the time he'd become an adult, he'd showered and shaved every day, and he'd gotten a haircut every two weeks. It had been almost a month since his last haircut, and he hadn't shaved yesterday.

He was beginning to spiral. The obsession was becoming unmanageable. But it was working. He had a connection to the woman in the Cage that was more than a logical tie. He cared about her, and that was what made things so much more difficult.

Instead of thinking of her as a tool that he admired, no different than a carpenter would take care of his favorite hammer, he thought of her as a part of himself. He'd become so inexplicably tied to her that at this point, he couldn't imagine his life without her.

The man ran his hand over the stubble on his chin. That was why he was so torn and twisted by the thought of continuing to force her to remain his captive. He had tried not to capture her to begin with. He'd kept several other women in this room prior to Cassandra, but he had never cared for them.

Then again, they'd been barely more than animals themselves by the end of the experiments, and when he'd disposed of them, he'd felt no more remorse than someone would feel when they disposed of the leftover food on their plate. If Cassandra ever became like they had, he was not sure that how he would handle it.

That was when he realized that maybe this time, he was the one becoming more animalistic, more out of control. And the thought scared him.

He leaned forward and looked into the emerald eyes in the mirror, searching for answers as a gypsy would look into a crystal ball. None waited for him except the obvious. Move faster. Be better. Trust Cassandra.

It was the same mantra he'd been telling himself for a long time. He took a deep breath and walked back into the viewing room. Cassandra sat on the floor naked again and the cat was lying next to her.

From the speaker came her voice. "Don't give me any more gifts. I won't use them. I want my cat, and I want the only gift left for you to give me, my freedom. Until then, none of the gifts matter."

It took the man only moments to get to his ready table and slide his shoes under the counter. He put the goggles on and flipped the switch.

For a split-second, he stood there, the door still closed and his chance to stop it all still an option. He knew that this would change everything. Talking to her was a bad decision, but she'd become his drug, his addiction. For the very first time in the man's life, he was not thinking rationally.

He walked to the door and unlocked it. He let it swing inward, and he stepped into the pitch-black room. He took a deep breath, not worrying about making a sound. He looked at the woman and the kitten who was already growling at him. Their images were no more than bits of colors making up a blurry picture of their real forms.

"Hello Cassandra. I think that it's time that we had a talk."

Chapter 36

"Did any cute boys give you Valentines?" Susan asked Cassandra quietly. Miss Franny wasn't home right now, but that didn't mean that there was a reason to tempt fate. *Silence was safety.*

"There were a few," she said with a bit of a smile. "But I don't know why. I don't talk to them." At twelve years old, Cassandra was just hitting puberty, and her body was changing, but her actions had not changed. She still stayed away from her male classmates.

"Because you're pretty, Cassandra. You've got such pretty hazel eyes and you're skinny, and you're starting to get boobs. Boys like boobs." Cassandra looked down at the ground. "But I don't like them. They want to do things like kiss, and kissing is stupid."

"Why do you think kissing is stupid? I happen to like it a lot." Cassandra looked at her sister in shock. "Who have you kissed?" she asked.

"I've kissed a few different boys," she said coyly. "None of them are boys you'd know, Cassandra."

"Well, if you're such an expert, then why do you like to kiss?" Cassandra asked with curiosity.

"Because it feels good. At least when they're good kissers. Not that nasty puppy dog kissing that some of them try. I don't want their tongues on my lips. That's gross. But when you can feel more than their lips, it's like magic. No, that doesn't make sense, does it. It's like you can touch their soul when you kiss them the right way. Like their body and your body don't matter so much anymore and it's just heat and lips and… and magic."

Cassandra gave Susan a confused look and shook her head. "Well I don't think I ever want to kiss a boy then. Boys don't have souls. They're demons. I don't think I want to touch a demon's soul." Susan laughed, unable to contain herself like soft crystal chimes in the otherwise silent house.

"I think I'll stick to them tempting me with chocolates," Cassandra said with a gleam in her eyes. She held up her bag of Valentine's candy and pulled out a piece of chocolate with the Valentine attached. She read the card and looked at Susan as she pulled it off.

"Sorry Steven, I don't think that you'll be touching my soul anytime soon." Susan laughed again, a sound that was rare in this house for unwanted children.

Joe came into the room. "What's so funny?" he whispered loud enough for them to hear him from across the room. "Come over here so we don't have to yell," Susan said as she laid down on the floor and let her bright red hair splay out over the wood.

He walked across the floor without making a sound, and Cassandra stood up, picking up her bag of Valentines. "I've got to go put my bag of candy up, and then I'm going to scrub the bathroom. Miss Franny will like that. I heard her acting funny about the bathroom this morning."

Joe and Susan followed Cassandra as she passed the door under the stairs. Before she passed it though, she pulled out a candy and bent down. She slid it under the door.

"Why'd you do that?" Joe asked. Susan said, "She always gives a piece of candy to Billy when she has extra. Didn't you know that?"

"Yeah, I knew that, but why do you do it? He never gives you any, and he's crazy. That's why he stays under the stairs all the time."

"He doesn't get any candy. Ever. He doesn't even get to play. I know he's supposed to be crazy, but if I ever go crazy, I hope that someone would slide a piece of candy under my door every once in a while. It would be better if he could come out and play, but I don't know where Miss Franny and Mr. George keep the key to the door."

"Yeah, but that's cause he's crazy. Miss Franny and Mr. George lock him away because they're scared of him. I hope that if I ever go that crazy that they just kill me and be done with it. I couldn't handle being locked away like that."

"I don't want to die. When he turns eighteen, they can't keep him. He just has to live another few years in there, and then he's free to do as he pleases. Miss Franny and Mr. George can't do anything to him after that." They all got quiet at the thought of how close they all were to getting out of the house.

Already, Paul, the oldest boy, had left. He came back once to say hi to all the kids that he'd grown up with, but Mr. George had tried to punish him, and he'd hit Mr. George in the face. He'd told him that he didn't have to listen to him anymore, and that if he ever tried to touch him again, that he'd kill him.

Paul hadn't come back after that, but the other kids were getting close. They were excited about it, but their excitement was dangerous. Miss Franny was already on edge because of how big they all were. It was hard for her and Mr. George to force the kids to do things, so they were even meaner than they used to be.

Cassandra had begun doing extra chores in her spare time so that Miss Franny would be happier, but it was beginning to be less effective. Just two days before, Joe had been punished by being forced to walk around in one of Susan's dresses.

He'd gotten scared when Mr. George had wanted him to climb onto the roof of the barn to clean off the leaves. There wasn't a ladder that reached the top, so Joe had to climb up the drain pipe. There were places you could put your feet, and no one had fallen before, but Joe was getting bigger and heavier, and he was scared that he'd break the footholds and fall the fifteen feet.

Mr. George had called him a little girl and had used the incident to prove his superiority by forcing Joe to wear the dress and a pair of Susan's panties for the rest of the day. Everyone was required to refer to Joe as a Josephine.

It had embarrassed Joe, but mostly it made everyone mad. There was no reason that Mr. George couldn't have just bought a ladder. He wouldn't have climbed the drainpipe and Joe weighed nearly as much as Mr. George now that he was fifteen years old.

It wouldn't be long before something really bad would happen. Cassandra could feel it in her bones, and so could everyone else. So Cassandra cleaned the bathroom before it was something that they could get into trouble for.

Her siblings continued to chat about their Valentine's day while Cassandra put her candy in her room and went to clean the bathroom. There was a fear that lingered in the air, and the others seemed to just ignore it, but Cassandra worked to keep the bad thing from happening. Whatever it was.

Chapter 37

45 days Since the Cage, Age 31

"Hello Cassandra. I think that it's time that we had a talk."

The words hung in the air. Cassandra had hoped to talk to him. She hadn't been sure what she would do if he actually came into the room, but she knew that the closer he was to her, the better. Maybe she'd be able to talk her way into release, but more likely, she'd have a better chance of trying to escape the Cage.

"Thank you," she said into the nothingness. She closed her eyes and pretended that she was just practicing her blind walking. It didn't help very much. Every sound seemed amplified inside the darkness, and when the Monster dragged the chair to a space in front of her, she shivered. He was looking directly at her. She knew that. She had no idea how he was seeing her, but he was.

"Cassandra, you say that you can help me more easily by talking. So do it. Talk to me and help me to understand you better."

His voice was cold and rough. His throat seemed parched, as though he hadn't had enough water. Cassandra shivered naked in the darkness. She hadn't expected it to be this intimidating.

She'd been naked for weeks now, and she'd known that he was watching her. Now, it was more than a cerebral knowledge. He was staring at her naked body in the darkness now. She felt so vulnerable.

"I don't know how to help you, but I know that talking through letters is less personal and less emotionally stimulating than face to face. Why don't we try just talking?"

Cassandra couldn't help but shiver as fear rolled off her in waves again. This man was terrifying, and she hadn't expected him to be. She'd felt confident when writing letters to him, but the fact that he had tortured and killed her boyfriend without feeling anything was at the forefront of her mind now.

The darkness didn't seem to bother her captor. He sat still for a few minutes, but then he got up, seemingly unable to stay seated for very long. She obviously couldn't see him, but she had been practicing visualizing what was happening through sound.

"Do you remember caring about anyone before?" she asked softly. Fear was almost tangible in the darkness, but she'd been this scared many times before. She could work through fear.

"No. Until the emotions I have felt recently, I have had no feelings towards another human or an animal." The air seemed pregnant with unspoken words. They both knew who he'd had feelings towards. He was embarrassed. Yet another emotion that he'd never had before. She was even more afraid. If he truly had emotions towards her, would he be able to let her leave? Ever?

"What about your parents? Can you tell me about your mother and father?" Cassandra asked, knowing the answers already. She'd taken enough psychology classes in college to know that a true psychopath would not feel an emotional connection to his parents.

"They don't matter, Cassandra, and you should not dwell on them. They died, and I didn't shed a tear. Psychologists I have spent far too much money on have focused much of their attention on this fact, but they found nothing of significance. I was born this way. My mother told me that I was born without a soul, and she would cry herself to sleep at night because of it."

She tried a different approach. "What about your childhood. Did you have any friends?"

The man chuckled. "No, I didn't have any friends, Cassandra. This isn't the right path. Don't try to understand me. You need to try to focus on the emotions, not on me."

She sighed and wished she was more capable of pacing the room in the dark. She was stuck sitting on the floor with the little cat in her lap.

"Then what do you think sadness is?"

"Sadness is a feeling of loss. It is the feeling one would have when someone they care about dies or leaves them permanently or even for a short time."

Suddenly, the man stopped. He stopped pacing. He stopped talking. Everything stopped. Cassandra tried to breathe as softly as possible so that she could hear him move in the nothingness.

"Is that what it is?" the man asked the nothingness. "Is that sadness?" He sounded insane talking to himself in the darkness. "Sadness is time without *her*."

"How would anyone live like that?" She heard him move in the darkness, and then she could feel him. His breath was so close. A foot away maybe.

"Is that what it felt like to lose your parents?" he said softly. The sound came from less than a foot away, and the voice seemed to boom even though it was no louder than a whisper.

Cassandra shook in fear. He was insane. It didn't matter if he was insane, though. She had to keep him from unleashing that madness on her. "Yes," she whispered back.

"How did you handle that pain as a child?"

"It was hard. It broke me. I've already told you. You were born broken, but there are many of us out there who have been broken since then."

"Oh." He moved back to his chair. He sat down for a moment, and they sat quietly together.

Then he moved again. He stood up and pulled the chair back to the desk. He walked back to where the chair had been, and he said, "You were right. We will do this every day, and for your trouble, I will bring you extra food. And extra food for your cat. Even if it is a terrible beast."

Then he was gone, and Cassandra felt the wind on her face as the door shut. She closed her eyes before the lights flashed back on.

Her captor was a madman, but she had gotten what she needed from him. He would come inside the room and talk to her. Maybe she could convince him to let her go. And if not…

Chapter 38

Cassandra,

You're helping me. The only thing that might help more would be your touch. I have craved it for a reason that is unknown to me. I have never craved a person's touch before, never wished to touch anyone other than for utilitarian reasons.

This is different. I am sure that I seem insane to you. Is that different than soulless? Is it better or worse? The poets would say that all emotion is insanity, and now that I've felt it, maybe I can agree with them. I am on this path for better or worse, though, and I thank you for your help.

I ask only that you continue to talk to me as you did today. It was terrible to feel even that imagined sadness. I cannot begin to guess how it would feel for you to witness your parents die. Looking back, I knew that you had felt sadness, that it was hard for children to bear the weight of the loss of their parents.

The difference is that I knew this as I know that that the arctic is cold and unbearable. I cannot imagine the cold of the arctic, cannot place myself there and understand the difficulty of the traveler. Yesterday, I could not put myself in your place as a child feeling this weight. Now I do, and I do not understand the strength that you had at such a young age.

Yet, once more I am experiencing new emotions. They seem to be crashing through me as though a dam had broken. Every few hours, a new emotion seems to wind its way through me as a realization.

I may have to concede that you were right when you told me you hoped that I did not ever find the end of my quest. Some of these emotions are physically painful. Why have I been considered broken? It seems that I was the one that was saner and more whole than the rest of society.

My question to you, "Why do you want to leave so badly if you find the world so terrible?"

Chapter 39

Cassandra lay on the bed in a half-awake state. Tigger was curled up in her arms as she slept. He'd gotten bigger in the six weeks since she'd gotten him. He was still very much a kitten, but he had begun to attack objects other than the woman he had claimed as his.

His purring calmed her body. Even though she had grown somewhat comfortable in her Cage, the knowledge that a madman loomed just outside of her room kept her in a constant state of awareness. Tigger was the only thing that managed to help her body calm down. She'd never been able to put her finger on what it was exactly, but it was a simple truth.

Her eyes were closed when the lights went off without a sound, but she knew it had happened immediately. Even through closed eyes, she could tell that the darkness had come, and with it, the Monster. The breeze blew, and she sat up. She closed her eyes, practicing her calmness.

Life had become very simplistic in the Cage. She either ate and wrote in the journal, slept, played with Tigger, or she practiced blind walking. Her captor had seen her do it. There would be no way to hide it from him. He may have understood what she was doing, or maybe he hadn't. It didn't matter. He hadn't stopped her.

She had decided that she was going to escape her Cage soon. Monster was becoming more and more fragmented and unraveled. She'd made him feel, but now he was beginning to show her that he wanted more, needed more than just simple feelings.

He was becoming dangerous in his madness, and though he hadn't hurt her yet, she was worried that he would change the terms of their agreement. If he did, then she would very possibly be stuck in the room for ever.

For now, though, she would still comply.

Cassandra heard the chair slide across the floor to stop in front of her bed. "Good evening, Cassandra," Monster said softly into the darkness. His voice was still gravelly, but the parched sound was gone. In its place was an intensity that hadn't been there before. He'd been uncertain before, but now, there seemed to be a clarity and a purpose.

"Good evening. Is there a name I can call you? I didn't want to waste a question on it while we were communicating only through the letters, but now that we're speaking, it might be nice to know your name."

Moments passed as Monster thought. "No, Cassandra. No, I think that it would be best if you didn't know my name. If you'd like, you can choose whatever name you'd like to call me."

She almost didn't say it, but she'd been calling him the name for nearly her entire captivity. "Monster."

"That's a fitting name, Cassandra, but I'm surprised that you'd be brave enough to use it."

"If you're truly a psychopath, you shouldn't be bothered by the term."

The man paused, caught off guard once again by her honesty and insight. "That's true. I guess that I can't hold that logic against you. Now, what will we talk about today?"

Cassandra had spent a fair share of time thinking about what she would talk to him about since yesterday. She'd come to a single conclusion. He was looking for a specific emotion. Otherwise, he would have already set her free. But first, she had a question.

"You said that you would free me when I taught you to feel. By your own hand, you've stated that you can feel, that you have felt emotions that you've never felt before."

"Have I not kept my end of the bargain? I have done everything that you requested of me. You can follow this rabbit hole of emotions to your heart's content, and I will be happy enough away from you." She sat quietly as she let him think on her words.

"You're right." He paused, and Cassandra let him work through his thoughts. He sighed and stood up to pace once again. This seemed to be his way to deal with difficult thoughts.

"You see, I *am* beginning to feel, but I worry that the moment that you leave, I will be stuck. You've been my emotional muse, not my emotional inspiration. Does that difference make sense?" Cassandra didn't respond. He was not finished.

He continued to pace, and Cassandra worked hard at pinpointing exactly where he was. She needed the practice. "I want to give you your freedom, Cassandra. I truly do. I just can't quite yet. It will happen soon, but I can't give you a date. I... I can't let you go yet. It's all too close. So close."

He turned to her, and Cassandra realized that she could tell where he was looking by the sound of his feet even on the muffling carpet. Cassandra began to pet Tigger.

"Let us revisit this topic in a week, Cassandra. By then, I should be able to tell you a better estimate on how long I will keep you."

"I understand," she said softly, obviously disappointed.

"It's not that I don't want to let you go. You know that, don't you?" he said in the darkness. It was almost as though she could see his eyes in the darkness, wishing and praying that she'd believe him. She didn't. Not by a long shot. Obsession is a dangerous thing, and this man was consumed by it.

"Yes, I understand." *Submission was safety.*

"Good. Then what do you think we should talk about today?" he asked.

"Love. You seem to wonder about it a lot." She pulled the blanket off her and stood up. Tigger meowed at her. This was the first time that she'd moved in the darkness before.

If he could pace, so could she.

"It's been on my mind regularly for a while now." His words were not quite so confident.

"What do you think about it?" She tried to push him towards the same reaction as he'd had yesterday.

"I think that it is the cause of much of the world's strife. Men go to war over it, and they spend their fortunes trying to find it. Women sacrifice themselves over and over again in hopes that they'll find it."

"Then, once these fools find it, they hurt their lovers and then their lovers hurt them. Over and over again, until they either die or find a new lover." His pacing continued, and Cassandra walked to the end of the bed, to the place that she could sit closest to him.

She was tempting him, forcing him to accept her presence and not just her voice. It worked, and he stopped pacing. His feet would have been too close to her for his comfort.

"Then why do they keep looking for it? Why does everyone keep looking?" she asked, keeping his mind on the question instead of the fact that she stood up and moved towards him.

"Because it is all consuming," he said. "An obsession." His voice became less confident, but more knowing as he focused more on Cassandra. "Once a man or woman allows it into themselves, they lose sight of everything else. The hormones flow through them, and nothing else matters as much as the object of their obsession."

"So love is obsession?" she asked as she took a step toward him. Her voice was soft in the darkness, not like a whisper, more like a breeze as it flowed through the monster.

"No," he said breathlessly. Cassandra felt like she could hear his heartbeat in the nothingness. The two of them were the only things that mattered in the world right then. The rapid beating of their hearts continued as she took one more step toward him.

Less than an arm length separated them now. "Love is *the obsession*. Drug addiction, family businesses, children, careers, and even wives have been ignored and forgotten in the name of love. Lives have been lost in pursuit of it. There is no other thing that consumes humans so much as love. Not even money and power."

Cassandra moved her arm outward. It was as though she could see the man in the darkness, and he didn't move away from her. She pictured him standing there. She had no idea what he would wear, no idea what he looked like. He was rough though. She knew that. His voice had told her that he was not a soft man.

When she brushed his hand, he didn't pull away. She put her hand into his, and said, "Like the way you've followed me and watched me?" Monster had touched her, but Cassandra had never touched him.

The hand pulled away from her, and the man was gone. The breeze blew, and the door was shut. When the lights turned back on, she was standing naked in the room alone. Tigger looked at her with his head cocked to the side. She shook her head softly and got back in bed.

Chapter 40

Monster,

I want to leave so that I can be free. The world may be terrible, and it may be filled with cruelty, but that doesn't mean that it is worse than a Cage. There is nothing worse than a Cage, not even death.

I do not know what death will bring, but the Cage brings nothing, and that is so much worse than anything I have ever found. I will gladly seek out my own death if that is the only alternative to the Cage.

You wanted to know what it would be like to touch me. It will change you. The difference between letters and voices is far less than the difference between voices and touches. Voices are how you find friendship. Touches bring emotion.

You aren't ready for that yet, though, are you? I know that you're hesitant to let this change happen. You're afraid. Stepping outside of your coldness is not an easy thing, and you barely have your toes in the pool of emotion right now.

If you're bound and determined to find out what it's like living with emotions, you'll have to do more than watch, read, and listen. You're right about that.

"Are you ready to feel?"

Cassandra Matheson

Chapter 41

Cassandra was in the bathroom when the lights turned off. She smiled as she wiped and stood up. Even in the darkness, she walked to the sink and washed her hands. She took in all of the noises, placing them in her mind. Soft feet on the carpet.

When she walked into the main room, Monster spoke to her. "I see that you've learned to move in the darkness."

"There's nothing else for me to do, Monster." She walked to the chair, moving inches away from him. He didn't get out of her way. There was no wind from his motion. She'd have known. She may not have been able to place where exactly he would be, but she'd have known that he'd moved.

"It's a valuable skill," he said. "Now, if you're going to sit in the chair, where do you expect me to sit?"

"I don't know. The bed? It's your Cage. Sit where you like." Monster chuckled at her confident reply and moved to the bed.

He stopped for a moment and they both heard the hiss. Monster had already seen the kitten, but he hadn't expected it to move in front of him in an effort to protect the bed.

"It seems that your beast does not like the idea of me on your bed," he said. He moved to the opposite wall near the pile of gifts that Cassandra had not used. Cassandra closed her eyes and viewed the room in her mind.

He sat down and said, "I apologize for my abrupt departure yesterday. I… I was surprised, and I did not believe that it was in either of our best interests for me to stay."

"You know that the more times you run off and leave things unfinished, the less likely you'll walk all the way through your emotions. Sometimes, you have to give up some control."

She stood up and began to pace. She could feel his eyes watching her as she moved back and forth across the room.

"Yes, Cassandra. I am well aware of how poorly I have been handling my emotions."

"It's frustrating," she said. Her feet kept the same exact rhythm as she crossed the room repetitively. Back and forth. Back and forth. The rhythm never changed. "The faster you learn, the faster I get to leave, Monster. If you care about me as you say you do, you'd work harder at it.

He didn't respond to her comment. "Would you like to talk about love again?" Monster asked as he watched her body through the goggles.

"Yes. I want you to tell me why you left. I touched you, and it made you leave. I assume it had something to do with your attraction to me." She paused for a moment. "Your obsession with me."

He stood up at her words. It was almost like she could feel him. Like there was an invisible connection between the two of them in the nothingness. When he shuffled his feet, she knew the pacing would begin. "I…" he turned away from her.

Silently, Cassandra picked up the chair without breaking her rhythm. Her feet steered her towards Monster instead.

"I think that…" he paused as though something had startled him. He swiftly turned. Cassandra heard the shift in his steps and knew what had happened. She gave up the rhythm. The game was up. Blindly, she charged Monster. She knew where he was, and she was only a few feet away.

It was now or never. She'd been caught in the motion, and he could see somehow. He knew where she was whether she moved or not. The chair would give her away, and she was only a few steps away from possible escape.

Time slowed down as her adrenaline pushed her awareness beyond her normal possibilities. Every sound registered a motion in her mind in the silence. The picture in her mind of the tiny world she'd memorized every detail to changed to fit the motion.

Then she felt the crunch. A sickening sound and feeling filled the room as she abandoned the charge and stumbled, doing her absolute best to keep from putting any more weight on him than she already had. There was only one thing in the room that she couldn't track through sound.

A loud screech filled the room as she heard Monster say, "Idiot woman," harshly before silence. The breeze passed as the door closed, and she was left alone in the Cage.

Chapter 42

16 years before the Cage, Age 15

"Susan, you can't be serious!" Cassandra exclaimed in an excited whisper as they walked into the dining room from the front door.

"Of course, I'm serious. You need to stop having such a prudish view on the world. It was funny when you called boys demons when you were younger, but Cassie, they're going to grow up and be men. And you're going to have to end up sleeping with them eventually."

"Of course, I'll end up sleeping with men, but these aren't men. They're boys. And why would I want to have sex with them? I don't even enjoy kissing them very much." Susan looked at the note again.

"Want to come out to the lake tomorrow night?"

It was code for, "Want to come out to the lake and do things that we wouldn't want our parents to know about." Cassandra knew that. Susan knew that.

"How would I even get out there? Miss Franny wouldn't ever let me go out." Susan stared at her in disbelief.

"Why don't just sneak out?" she whispered.

"No! Do you know how bad I'd get punished for that if Miss Franny caught me?" Susan snorted. "Miss Franny's getting old, Cassie. It's time that we stopped being so worried about what she'd do to us."

"Oh, is she?" Miss Franny said as she stepped out from around a corner. Both of the girls stared in horror at her. Susan may have talked a big game, but pure and unadulterated terror flowed from her.

"What are you two little sluts planning?" she asked with a bit of a snarl as she walked towards the two girls.

"Nothing, Miss Franny," Cassandra said quickly. She glanced at Susan out of the corner of her eye. Susan quickly added, "No, Miss Franny. We weren't planning anything at all."

"That's good. It sounded a lot like you were planning to meet some boys tomorrow." Her lips curved up in a devious smile, showing just a bit of teeth.

"No, I was just saying that I wouldn't want to do that is all," Cassandra said, her eyes wide with terror.

"I know, Cassandra. You've always tried to do what Mr. George and me wanted." She looked pointedly at Susan. "This little slut, though…" She looked at Susan and saw the note in her hand.

"What's this?" she said quickly as she snatched the note out of her hand. "If you didn't want to go, then why did you keep the note?" she snarled accusingly.

Susan began to shake. "I… I…"

"That's what I thought. You little slut." She moved as fast as lightning as she reached out and grabbed Susan by the hair. Her hand tangled itself in the hair at the top of her head, and she yanked her forward toward her bedroom.

"George!" she screamed in anger. Cassandra heard them meet up between the dining room and their bedroom. Hushed whispers were exchanged and then they both went into their bedroom dragging Susan with them.

For a moment, Cassandra couldn't move. Her feet felt nailed to the floor as her stomach sunk. No one was punished alone. No one was punished in the bedroom.

She didn't know what to do. Things had gotten so much worse over the past few years. The beatings didn't hurt the older kids like they had when all of the kids were young. Mr. George wasn't strong enough to keep the kids in line, and after Paul had punched him, he'd been hesitant to put Joe in line with physical force.

They'd begun getting more creative and more cruel. Cassandra was the youngest of the bunch, but Susan seemed to get the most punishments. Maybe it was her attitude or maybe it was just the fact that she had red hair. People seemed to dislike people with red hair and freckles like Susan.

Cassandra began to breathe faster. She didn't know how to help. Joe was the only boy left, and he wasn't around to help Susan. Susan started screaming from the bedroom. The kids didn't scream like they used to. They'd learned about pain in this house.

Pain was temporary. Cassandra had been beat enough times that she could leave the pain behind and get lost in her own mind. She wouldn't scream. It would let Miss Franny and Mr. George win.

So why was Susan screaming now? And why was she screaming, "Help!"? All of the children knew that there was no one to help them in this house. Yet, Susan was still begging and screaming.

Cassandra couldn't handle it anymore. She raced into the kitchen and got a knife. Then she ran to Miss Franny and Mr. George's door. They had been so confident that no one would do anything that they hadn't even bothered to lock the door.

She burst through it wielding the twelve-inch chef's knife. Her hand shook as she looked in at a scene that would haunt her as much as the collapsed room had.

Miss Franny stood beside the bed with a smirk on her face. She leaned forward with her arms supporting her as she looked at Susan's face as tears streamed down it. Only inches away, she was watching with a joyous satisfaction. Susan hadn't screamed because of a punishment like this in years.

Susan was bent over the side of the bed as though she were getting a spanking. That wouldn't have been unusual. At least one of the children received a spanking for something every three or four days. No one would have screamed, and nothing would have been said. That was simply the life they had all grown accustomed to.

This was different. Her dress had been pulled up and draped over her back. Both of her hands were being held behind her back by Mr. George with one hand. Her legs were spread, and her panties had been pulled down to her ankles.

She turned to look at Cassandra with tears streaming down her face. Mr. George stood behind her with his pants around his ankles as well. Although Cassandra couldn't see exactly what was happening, she knew what was going on.

She didn't hesitate. The adrenaline that had flowed through her when she'd decided that she would help Susan pushed her to action. Step by step, time slowed down as she raised the knife above her head and charged Mr. George.

But she was a child still. Fifteen years old with a petite body. Mr. George turned to the side and caught her arm as she swung. The blade grazed his shoulder as he turned to catch her arm.

Cassandra watched as the thin stream of blood began to flow from his skin and she pushed with all her might to force the blade against his chest, but his grip on her arm was too strong. He was too strong.

He held her hand still with his right hand, and he pried the knife out of her grasp with the other. As soon as the knife was out of her hand, Miss Franny came up behind her and screamed, "You've done it now, idiot girl. There's only one thing we can do now."

She grabbed Cassandra by the hair just as she had done to Susan only moments before. She dragged Cassandra behind her, completely ignoring her futile attempts to untangle her hands from her hair. Through the dining room, and into the hall, she forced Cassandra to the door under the stairs.

For the first time ever, Miss Franny opened the door with a key from her pocket. Cassandra looked at the room that Billy, the boy she'd never seen, had lived in. She looked at the plastic bucket in the corner that had stains from urine and feces. She saw the cot with only a sheet where the boy had slept. There was nothing else in the room.

And Miss Franny threw her into the room. When she shut the door, Miss Franny yelled, "And you'll stay there until you've learned your lesson!"

Cassandra sat on the cot. The only light in the room came from the crack under the door. She shivered. Everything was quiet now. She could have been worried about herself, could have worried about what would happen to her now, but instead, she only thought of Susan, only worried that Susan would be raped even though she'd tried her best.

She just wasn't strong enough. There had been nothing she could have done differently. She was too slow, too weak. And she'd failed Susan. She sat on the cot and began to cry in the darkness.

She heard the screams then. She stood up and tried to open the door, but it was locked tight. She'd known it would be, but she'd had to try.

The screams went on and on. Cassandra beat on the raw wood of the door until her hands bled as she cried and screamed in solidarity. She hated Miss Franny, and she hated Mr. George. But more than anything, she hated that she couldn't do anything to help Susan.

Chapter 43

The lights had come back on last night. Cassandra didn't know when it had been. There hadn't been food then, and there hadn't been a letter either. She'd made a terrible mistake yesterday. She'd been wrong about so many things.

She'd thought that nothing could be worse than waiting for Monster to let her out. She'd been wrong. Waiting for her punishment was worse. Waiting without Tigger was worse. More than anything, knowing that she hurt Tigger was worse.

Cassandra had never owned a pet. She'd never grown up with them before, so there had been no desire to get one as an adult, and they seemed like an awful lot of work. Playing with Tigger, watching him grow, and watching him decide that he loved her had been different than she'd ever expected.

Monster had given the cat to her as his way of giving her an outlet for her desire to help the helpless. She understood that. She couldn't have let him starve, so she'd given him some food. She'd done the same with all of the abused children. The difference was that she'd never become attached to those kids.

She'd become attached to Tigger. That little shit had saved her from insanity. She knew what it was like to be in a cage all alone, and the weeks in this one had not been anywhere nearly as bad as it could have been because of the little fluffball.

His insane antics and constant need to attack anything that moved had given her more smiles and laughs than she would ever find in her Cage without him. Even if she stayed in the Cage for the rest of her life, she'd never smile as much as she had in the six weeks with Tigger.

Last night, she'd cried herself to sleep. It had been the first time that she'd cried since she'd become an adult. She'd made it through Craig's murder without shedding a tear. Admittedly, he wasn't the best boyfriend, but they'd been together for a year.

She loved Tigger. She would have to amend her list of people she loved from four people to four people and one idiot kitten. And now he was gone because she'd made a mistake. Because she'd hurt him.

She'd heard and felt the crunch and the mewling that had come from the kitten. He'd never made that kind of noise before. He was so little. So fragile. And now he was hurt.

The lights shut off, and instead of fear, Cassandra felt hope. Maybe she'd hear news about Tigger. Maybe Monster would bring him back. She'd take any punishment if that's what it took to save the kitten. She knew that. She'd let him do anything to her if it meant that the kitten would be safe and back with her.

When the lights came back on, though, there was no kitten, and there was no Monster. Only a tray of food with no letter to accompany it. Cassandra began to cry again, and she ignored the tray of food. She couldn't eat. Not then.

She'd hurt the only living thing that she loved, and the heartache that coursed through her was more painful than any pain that Monster could punish her with.

Chapter 44

48 Days Since the Cage, Age 31

Cassandra tossed and turned. Anger had begun flowing through her consistently. She was powerless. Completely and utterly unable to do anything to help the kitten, unable to escape her Cage, unable to do anything.

The anger pulsed in her even as she slept. Nothing had happened. There had been no target of her rage, and there had been no way to express herself. She'd muttered and cursed, and at one point she'd even lost herself to the rage.

She'd turned on the pile of gifts and begun destroying them, one at a time. The dresses were shredded. The books had their pages ripped out. She hung onto the end of the cord of the vibrator and swung it against the wall, putting little holes in the drywall where it landed.

But the objects that she destroyed didn't relieve the rage that boiled inside of Cassandra. She wasn't sure why she felt the need to destroy things, but at the very least, she'd hoped that her Monster would come back to punish her. She needed someone to hate because right then, she hated herself more than anyone in the world.

Finally, after strewing her pile of destroyed gifts around the room, she'd collapsed on her bed and fallen asleep with tears still on her cheeks.

She woke up to darkness. Her body had been trained to acknowledge the darkness, so even if she was sleeping, she'd awaken to that sudden nothingness. She tried not to move, waiting to see whether Monster was coming to punish her or something else.

The lights turned back on, and she was up and out of bed instantly as she scrambled to the little blue cage that had been set next to the desk. Cassandra's heart pounded in her chest as she looked between the wires, scared of what she'd find.

Inside the cage was Tigger who seemed to be sleeping. She pulled him out of the cage and held him to her face. He purred lightly against her cheek, not waking up. She moved him away from her face to get a look at him, and she didn't see anything different other than his obvious sleepiness.

"I'm so sorry, Tigger." Tears streamed down her face, getting his fur damp as she held him against her cheek again.

He shifted in her hand, and she pulled him away. His eyes opened, and he hissed at her before scratching her cheek, not quite drawing blood. Then he closed his eyes again and began to purr. She put him to her breast and stood up. On the table, two bottles of pills and the journal sat.

She didn't want to look at them, didn't want to know what her punishment would be or how badly Tigger was hurt. She didn't want to know what her mistake had cost either of them. But she had to know. It wasn't in her to be a coward or to let fate decide something that she could have some control over.

Cassandra didn't set her kitten down, and instead simply worked with a single hand while the other held Tigger. She opened the notebook and took a breath.

She blamed herself. And for the first time, she was thankful to her Monster. He had done this for her. He hadn't needed to. She had been trying to kill him, and he'd saved her kitten in return. Knowing him like she did now, this was not something he would do for himself.

It was hard to start reading the notebook. Her mind had already come up with a thousand different horrible things she would find in the journal the next time she saw it.

She looked down at Tigger, his little body curled up to her skin. He was okay. She had told herself that she'd have done anything to make sure that he was safe. She'd meant it. She still meant it. If it was between keeping the furball safe and keeping herself safe, it was very likely she'd save the cat, however illogical that would be to most people.

Her entire life, she'd stayed safe. She had made sure that she survived. Silence was safety. Distance was safety. Submission was safety.

Things had changed. Tigger had changed her. Survival came second to love. It was a strange realization.

She still blamed herself for Tigger being hurt, and a part of her realized that Monster was the reason he was okay. That's when she decided she had to read the journal.

Chapter 45

Cassandra,

I could not write you a letter yesterday as I did not know what to say. As I'm sure you have assumed, I brought the kitten to the vet immediately after I left. He looked to be in a significant amount of pain, and I did not know how to fix him. He couldn't walk correctly, and his legs looked wrong, *like they'd been bent at the wrong angles.*

I told the vet that he'd gotten under foot and I stepped on him. I told him that I heard something crack, and that I was afraid I'd broken something, so he took X-rays.

He didn't have any broken bones. It is good that you didn't finish your charge, or it's likely he would have had many. Instead, his back two legs were dislocated. The vet put them back into place, and it seemed to help with his pain. All of that happened two days ago. The vet gave him drugs to help him sleep and for the remainder of the pain.

The vet kept him overnight in case there were internal injuries, but in the morning, he still couldn't move his back legs and was dragging them around behind him as he crawled. The vet told me that it was possible that there was damage to the spinal cord or some other nerve damage due to swelling.

I didn't want to write the letter telling you that. The vet said that it would either subside in 24 hours or it probably wouldn't ever get better. So, I did not write to you yesterday, as I know that you are fond of the creature regardless of the number of times that he attacks you.

This morning, I went back, and Tigger was walking around and snarling at everyone just like normal. The vet put him back on pain pills and a depressant to keep him from injuring himself. That is what the two bottles are. Please give him one pill in the morning and one pill in the evening from each bottle.

The dislocation most likely pinched nerves in his hips and caused him to be unable to move them. As the swelling went down, the nerves were released, and he became mobile again. The damage should not have any lasting effects. Though, in the future, I'd suggest you minimize stepping on him.

I'm sure that the creature's health was of the utmost concern to you, but there are things that we need to talk about, and I do not trust myself in the room with you currently. You tried to attack me. I understand that. You want out, and I hold the key. There will be no punishments, for you did not break a rule. You acted no differently than I would have, and I fully expected it. I have watched you try to walk in darkness for many weeks.

The entire experience has made it clear to me that you deserve your freedom. More than I initially believed possible, I feel like it would be painful for me to keep you locked up any longer. I am willing to cut our time together short for you.

There are still things that are missing, though. Pieces of my burgeoning soul that I inexplicably believe will wither and die if you leave now. I know that this is not your concern any longer, but in the spirit of complete honesty, I feel compelled to tell you.

It is difficult for me to comprehend the transformation that has begun to overcome me, but it seems completely limited to things involving you. You may have been right. Maybe my obsession is love. Maybe even a soulless being such as myself can find love.

I wish that things could have continued a different way, but it seems that our paths may be diverging soon. I would like you to stay here with me for another two days while the cat heals. Once you are released, you will be overwhelmed by reporters and police officers trying to capture me and trying to make money off your story. It will be better for the cat if you stay just for those two days while he recovers.

Monster

Chapter 46

Monster,

Thank you for taking care of Tigger. You have no idea how much it means to me that instead of being angry with me and taking that anger out on him, you had him treated.

I cannot completely forgive you for abducting me. I don't know if I ever will. You have not been a cruel jailor, but you have taken my life from me for many weeks now with no benefit to myself. I promised you that I would be truthful, so I will not keep anything from you. You deserve that at least.

I would prefer to leave today, but I do not disagree that my release will be a strain on both Tigger and myself. I will not argue with staying for two more days. It seems more than reasonable.

I do not believe you to be soulless. Broken, maybe. Different, certainly. But not soulless. You have done me kindnesses which do not benefit you in the least. That is not the mark of a man that is soulless.

My dear Monster, I do not know what I can do for you in that time, but I will give you whatever help you can think of in your quest for discovering your soul. When I fell that day, I didn't believe that I would ever see Tigger again. Though most people would see my fondness for him to be ridiculous, he has brought me more joy in mere weeks than anyone or anything has brought me in years.

I cannot explain the debt of gratitude I feel towards you, but as the smallest bit of repayment, I will not refuse any requests you have of me. I do not have anything else to give. "How can I help you?"

Cassandra Matheson

Chapter 47

The dress was torn this time. A rip ran up the side, passing through several patches in the green and white dress. Tears hadn't fallen from her hollow eyes in days. They wouldn't fall again for a very long time.

Tears were worthless things. You gave them to someone who did not deserve them. A tribute for the one who hurt you, who left you, or who terrified you. Cassandra had no more use for them. Her sadness had left her after the second day. No one was left in her world to deserve sadness.

Anger was all that was left to her. White hot and simmering under the skin. Waiting to find an outlet, a body to unleash it on.

Pain had its place too. A friendly reminder that she wasn't dead, and that there was still time to hurt the ones that had hurt her. It coiled in her groin and backside, throbbing and aching.

Mr. George had been rougher than normal this time. He'd put it in both holes. Cassandra had found solace in her safe spot, the place in her mind that she could go to when the world was too much for her fifteen-year-old mind to endure. A place of greens and whites and blues. A place of life and happiness, where all of her good memories lay.

The pain could rip through her body while she lay in that safe spot, and she wouldn't know that it was happening. When the hurting was done, she'd return and find the familiar ache that told her that she still had time to hurt them, to kill them if possible.

At first, she hadn't gone to the safe spot. She'd fought them. She'd kicked Mr. George in his spot twice in the first two weeks. She'd aimed for it, enjoying the way that he fell over moaning when she'd managed to hit her target. She'd been beat before he raped her each of those times, but it had been worth it. Her pain didn't matter. She would hurt regardless of what happened. But *his pain* was glorious.

That was all that waited for her every day. The door opened. She was yanked out into the light. They dragged her to the bedroom, and Mr. George would use her. Then she'd be thrown back into the room under the stairs.

Mr. George and Miss Franny seemed to enjoy it more if she hurt when he used her like that. Miss Franny had even started rubbing herself while she watched. She would hike up her dress when Cassandra began screaming.

Cassandra didn't understand any of it. All of it hurt her. Her whole body hurt, and no part of it was enjoyable, but she remembered a time where people had talked about it being enjoyable, about it being fun. Susan had said something along those lines.

Mr. George did all sorts of things to her after he had her pressed against the bed. He would spank her, and he would kiss Miss Franny. He would use one hole and then he would use the other. It didn't matter to her anymore. They both always hurt so much.

He never tried to make her use her mouth though. Cassandra had heard about boys who'd had girls use their mouth on them, but Mr. George wasn't that stupid. She'd have bit down as hard as she could if she'd been given the chance. Even if they'd beat her to death afterwards, it would have been worth it.

She fantasized about that sometimes. The way that it would go from hard to soft as the blood flowed and Mr. George screamed. She had initially thought of how he'd look as she spit it out on the ground. Cassandra had a lot of time to think about things, and then she remembered that doctors could reattach things.

She wouldn't let them reattach anything. She knew that if she bit it off, she wouldn't spit it out no matter how bad it tasted. She would chew and chew and chew it up into tiny little pieces. She would spit it out as a pile of goo as he screamed and they both hit her.

Then she would fantasize about them hitting her until she died. She imagined how good it would feel to be free of all the pain. She imagined the freedom of being away from Mr. George and Miss Franny. Even if she was dead, where ever dead was, it would be better than the room under the stairs and the bedroom where they would hurt her every day.

She'd almost tried to find a place to hurt herself. She knew that if she started bleeding bad enough, she'd die. She'd looked around and found plenty of nails that would work, but then she thought of Susan out there. If she died, who would take the pain?

Mr. George had gotten a taste for her. It seemed that he wasn't the decent man she'd thought he was at first. It wouldn't end any time soon. She knew that. He and Miss Franny liked it too much. Cassandra could tell that they enjoyed themselves. Especially when it hurt. If she wasn't there, they would hurt Susan instead. She couldn't imagine Susan going through it. Susan didn't have a safe spot like Cassandra did. Susan still cried.

It all seemed so long ago. The days seemed like eternities sitting in that room doing nothing except listening to the rest of the people in the house. She heard everything. Mr. George and Miss Franny talking about all manner of things including herself, and she heard more than anything, the times that the others would get punished.

The door opened, and Miss Franny stood in the doorway. "I don't think you should be allowed out of there yet, but Mr. George says that he thinks you've learned your lesson. Have you learned your lesson, idiot girl?"

Time slowed as Cassandra stared at Miss Franny. She wanted to kill the woman. She wanted to take her make-up covered face and bash it into the wall over and over again. There was absolutely nothing that she wanted more than that. There was only one thing that stopped her.

She'd tried to attack Mr. George before, and that was how she'd wound up under the stairs. She'd been too weak and too slow. She didn't even have a weapon now.

"Yes, Miss Franny," she said. She couldn't keep the anger out of her voice, but she could say the right words.

"Good. You'd better watch yourself though. If you try to do anything stupid like you did with that knife, you'll end up back in here again. Instead of two weeks, you'll stay here until you age out, just like Billy did. Do you hear me?"

"Yes, Miss Franny." That was all that Cassandra could say. Her hands twitched as she forced her body away from its desperate desire to attack the woman.

"Your punishment isn't done either. You're being let out of your cage. That's all." Now Cassandra understood. The rapes weren't going to stop, and if she fought, she'd end up back in the cage.

"Yes, Miss Franny." Her words were hollow, but they did the job. Miss Franny stepped out of the way for her, and she left the cage under the stairs.

"Go get changed. That dress is disgusting. Then you can come back downstairs and get to work." She nodded and went upstairs to her and Susan's room.

When she got there, all of Susan's stuff was gone. Her clothes were the only ones hanging in the closet, and Susan's bed was stripped of its bedding. Cassandra was confused, but she was so numb that she couldn't think about the possibilities of what had happened to Susan.

She came downstairs in a different dress, and Joe was coming in from the farm. "Heya Cassie!" he said as he ran up to her. "They said they weren't going to keep you there forever. Just a little while as a punishment. Guess you did something pretty bad, huh?"

She stared at him for a few seconds. Why hadn't he helped her? Why hadn't he done the same thing that she'd done? Joe was big now. He could have stopped Mr. George. She looked at his muscles, muscles he had earned working on the farm. He hadn't done anything even after she had screamed over and over again for two weeks. She'd begged for help. She'd screamed rape. He'd had to have known what was happening, and he'd ignored it.

"Where's Susan?" she asked, ignoring his questions.

"Guess you wouldn't know, huh? Susan ran off. That day that you and her got in trouble, well, she went up to her room after her punishment and we all thought she'd gone to sleep. But she didn't. She packed up some clothes and stuff, and she ran off without telling any of us where she was going."

So Cassandra had tried to save her, and instead of doing the same for her, Susan had run away and left her to her fate. So much for family. So much for trust. So much for protecting the people that mattered.

She looked at Joe and she shook her head softly. Something inside of Cassandra broke. It should have hurt. It was a sharp and jagged breaking, like her soul had been glass and life had hit it over and over and over again. Finally, that glass had shattered. It should have hurt. She should have fallen over, gasping in pain.

But she didn't. She didn't feel anything. She hadn't broken because Mr. George and Miss Franny had raped her and kept her in a lightless closet for two weeks. She hadn't broken when she'd been taken from Miss Faith and Big Tony. She hadn't broken when she'd watched her parents die in that fire.

She'd broken when her family had abandoned her. She'd shattered when Joe had acted like it was nothing. She'd shattered when Susan had run away after Cassandra had tried to save her.

She'd broken when she realized there was no one in the world that she could trust. And that realization was soul shattering.

Chapter 48

Cassandra,

There is only one thing that may help. I have tried to convince myself not to commit the thought to paper, but I have promised my honesty.

You may call me Monster, but I do not believe that I have earned the title from you. What I ask of you may make me one, though. If that is the case, I hope that you will refuse me regardless of your feelings of gratitude. I cannot bear the thought of hurting you more than you have already been hurt by everyone in the world.

I have thought on this topic for hours, and the only thing that I can imagine helping my quest to find my soul is to make love to you. The thought and desire has been on my mind for weeks now. I believe that you were correct when you told me that my obsession was love. I don't know what to do with the information, but something about it seems to hold the key to everything.

If we trust the poets, the translators of emotion throughout time, we would be led to believe that physical intimacy is the highest form of love that man can achieve. You yourself told me that touch is the key to it all.

I will not rape you. I will not force you or even make you feel indebted to me. I will not be a monster. I will not be like the rest of the world.

Although I hesitate to ask, the only question on my mind is, "Will you make love to me?"

Monster

Chapter 49

Monster,

    I will gladly give you my body. I knew that this would come eventually. This is not a surprise but speaking more of it will not do either of us any favors.

    Bring me a blindfold with my breakfast, and I will wear it. Tell me what to do, and I will do it. You do not need to worry about whether I will try to look at you. I still maintain enough self-preservation to prevent me from signing my own death warrant.

    You are a monster. You have claws and teeth, and you have not been afraid to use them. The important thing is that you have chosen not to use them on me, and that makes all the difference. Not all monsters are evil.

    "What will you do now that you have emotions?"

                             Cassandra Matheson

Chapter 50

Cassandra held the black silk in her fingers and slowly let it rub against her skin. She was thoughtful today. She would be free tomorrow. Tigger didn't need any more medication, and he didn't seem to be hurting too badly with how aggressive he was being towards the pile of scraps where her gifts had been.

Cassandra had cleaned the debris of her anger-fueled rampage. The Cage didn't have the clean feeling of a hotel room anymore. There was no sterility left in the room. She'd brought life to the room in its destruction. Holes pock-marked the walls, and bits and pieces of the clothes and books still lay embedded in the carpet.

She'd done what she could, but there was no way to revert the room back to the way it had been before she'd exploded. You could not take the life away from the room again. Anger had always been her strongest emotion. It didn't come out very often, but when it did, it was explosive.

She looked at the blindfold again and realized just how naked she was. Her nudity had become common and completely normal for her. She'd been naked for weeks, and initially, it had been strange, but she'd quickly gotten over it. Things had changed when he'd started coming into the room, when they'd begun talking. Now it was a constant thought.

Monster was watching her. He was always watching. The difference was that now he was going to turn out the lights, and she would put on the blindfold. Then, for the first time since she'd come into the Cage, he would turn the lights back on.

The thought of him seeing her and touching her made her feel strangely. He knew everything about her. He'd never actually hurt her even though he could. Even now, when she had offered him anything, he had seemed reluctant to accidentally hurt her.

Up until the last week, she'd thought of him as Monster because he'd been the monster waiting in the darkness, capable of anything, but now… now it seemed like she was more of a monster than he was. He had only ever committed one crime against her: her abduction and maintained captivity.

Cassandra struggled with maintaining her distance. She'd never had that problem before. She'd always distanced herself from Craig, never letting him get too close.

Then again, none of them had understood her. For all that Monster had said that he was trying to understand her, he already knew her better than anyone else in the world. He knew her favorite foods, he knew her past, and now he knew that there was only one creature that she cared about.

He'd understood her so well before he'd abducted her. He'd known how to capture her. He'd known more about her boyfriend than even she had known. He'd spent years watching. And helping?

Cassandra began to wonder what else he'd done for her. For her entire captivity, Cassandra had thought of his meddling in her life as a singular event, that Craig's murder was the only time he had influenced her life. Now though, she wondered how often he'd stepped in from the shadows and manipulated something in her favor.

She was in the middle of that train of thought when the lights shut off. Tigger was asleep in her arms, and she whispered to him, "You've got to sleep in your cage for a little while."

Standing up and moving to the cage was easy enough for her. She'd been ready to assault Monster only days before. She felt the breeze. He was in the room with her now. She walked back to the bed and put on her blindfold before taking a breath and saying aloud, "I have the blindfold on, Monster."

Seconds passed silently, and then she saw the light come back on through the blindfold. Cassandra lay in the twin bed with the white sheets and didn't shake. She was not afraid of this monster. Not anymore.

When he came to her, he did not come to her as a monster. There were no claws and teeth. He stood before her and let his hand move across her lightly tanned skin. He noted then how it had paled during her captivity. The hair that the man touched stood up as his finger grazed it.

He'd been with enough women to know that her body was reacting to his touch, and it meant nothing more than physical response. That brought him sadness. More than he'd expected, her lack of a response, her lack of desire, hurt him.

His fingers moved from her stomach to her breasts, circling her nipples and he watched them harden. He felt his own body's desire begin to stir. His fingers closed around her breast, squeezing softly as he bent down to kiss her other breast, leaving the barest hint of wetness behind.

His hand moved from her breast to her neck, and he watched the woman shiver under him. "You're beautiful," he said softly to the woman who lay on the bed. He had a hard time believing it was really Cassandra Matheson, his lifelong obsession that lay on the bed in front of him.

He'd seen her body so many times through the lens of a camera, that it did not excite him. Yet, he was excited now. He was seeing her differently now. She was not a woman to watch or learn from. She was a woman. She was *the woman*, and she was beautiful. A piece of art.

No. That was the way he would have thought of her before. It was not the sight of her that excited him. No, it was the fact that she was laying her emotions bare to him. He could tell from the way that her body moved, the way her breath changed that she was allowing herself to feel. And that was more than she'd done for anyone else.

He bent down to kiss her lips. Slightly pink and so full of life. Full lips that kissed back. She moved her hand to the back of his head and pulled him down to kiss her harder. Her tongue slipped into his mouth, and he felt himself losing control of the situation.

The monster wanted to run. He was a creature of the dark, and with the lights on, the woman was not so afraid of him.

The man wanted to stay though, and as he gave up that control, he let the woman who had become his everything guide him through this just as she'd guided him towards the soul he'd sought out.

Cassandra pulled Monster to him, forcing him to stop speaking. He was a thinker, a talker. He didn't need that. He had no more need for words. He needed her touch, and she needed his.

She admitted that to herself. He, the man who had abducted her and forced her into a Cage, was not a monster like the many men whom she'd met and been hurt by. She needed to give him this, and a part of her needed it too. She needed to know what it was like to really touch a man who had no desire to hurt her.

She'd been told that kissing was like touching a man's soul, and until today, she'd always thought it was simply a poetic euphemism because touching lips wasn't romantic enough. She'd been wrong. Until today, that's all it had been, but for the first time, she felt this man. All of him.

The man's hands ran from her neck to her cheek as he leaned down over her. She wanted to feel more than just his hands and his lips. She wanted his weight on top of her. She reached out and felt his body, naked and ready for her.

She whispered between kisses, "Lay on top of me." His body covered hers as he wrapped his arms under her and lay on top of her. His lips found new places to kiss her, going from her lips to her neck to her breast.

She moaned and let her body feel all of it, all of *him* as he explored her. She arched her back as he found her nipple with his kisses. "You're more than just beautiful Cassandra. You're... everything..."

She didn't respond. He found her opening and she knew that she was ready for him. Wetness ran between her legs as he spread her with his fingers, a shiver running through her body. Cassandra reached out and pulled him to her, forcing him to sheath himself inside her.

The man moaned above her as he filled her. He held himself up with one arm as he cradled her cheek in his other hand. He leaned down to kiss her again. Rough lips pressed against hers, and she felt his need. It wasn't a physical need. He wasn't horny, and he didn't need to "get off".

He needed *her*. It was that minute variation that made all the difference. This man had followed her through her life. He'd given up who knew how many opportunities he had as he watched her. And this was the crescendo of it all. He'd dreamt of this. And truth be told, she had as well.

They moaned together as he slowly rocked in and out of her. She'd never felt like this before. Sex had been a thing that people did to relieve an itch or to have fun. It had never been like *this*. No one had ever *needed* her, not for her body, but for the woman inside.

She ground her hips against his as he thrust harder, more filled with need. His kisses were harder, more insistent. She kissed him back just as harshly. They were broken, both of them, but in this moment, something changed.

They both needed each other right then. And neither of them had ever needed anyone before. He needed to know what it was like to be inside *her*, not just a woman, and she needed to know what it was like to be needed as a human, not as a tool.

Her lips left his as she leaned up, straining to find his throat. She kissed him roughly, and then she bit him. The sharpness of her teeth against his flesh spurred him into motion as he moaned loudly.

"Cassandra…" he said softly as he felt her tighten around him. Her hips gyrated as fast as they could under him, and he sped up.

"Monster…" Waves of pleasure rolled through her as she released his flesh and leaned back and let the orgasm overcome her.

He gripped her shoulders tightly and began to force her body against his as he pistoned in and out of her. She began to scream in pleasure as she gave her control to him.

He grunted softly as he felt his own release. His body relaxed, and he let the passion leave him as he took deep breaths while still looking down at Cassandra in amazement. He'd never expected anything to be like this.

Something had changed inside of him. He knew it as much as when she'd touched him. Except that this was different. That had been discovering that maybe his soul was broken, but it was still there. The pieces were still hidden in there, and he could touch them and feel them.

But they were still only pieces. He was still broken. This was more like some of those pieces had clicked together. The man took a deep breath and let it out slowly. Cassandra felt his breath on her face, and she shivered.

The man climbed off her and as he stood next to her, he ran his hand across her bare stomach. Cassandra reached up to touch his chest and felt soft hair. She ran her fingers through it.

"Thank you, Cassandra," he said softly, and then she felt him melt away. She felt the door close, and she took a deep breath before taking off the black silk blindfold.

"I'll miss you, Monster," she said softly to the empty room.

Chapter 51

Cassandra,

I have no idea what I will do now that I can feel. I will most likely try to find some other kind of meaning in the world, but I do not know how successful I will be. My life has been simple since I was a child, and I feel very lacking in direction currently.

I've put some thought into it, and I think that maybe I will try to find something that will help people to fill my time. It still doesn't make very much sense to me to help other people, but I don't know what else to do.

I will miss you Cassandra. I hope that the past months have not been the worst you have ever endured, and I wish that I could have made it enjoyable enough for you to want to stay longer.

I will miss our chats, and I will miss our letters. You've done more for me than anyone has. You have cared more than anyone has, and you've shown me kindness when it was unnecessary.

I hope that you live a happy life with your kitten. Don't let it get fat. It would be a terrible thing to see him unable to pounce on toes.

I've placed a cupcake on the desk. A celebratory cupcake. If you eat it, you'll magically wake up on your doorstep with a snarly kitten next to you. I will be sad to see you go, but I gave my word. You've helped me to feel something, and I will fulfill my end of the bargain.

I don't have any questions for you, my dear Cassandra. Goodbye.

Monster

Chapter 52

Cassandra looked around the Cage. She noted the holes in the spackled wall and thought about the crumbled drywall under her bed. The pile of trash in the corner of the room was just another memory that she'd carry with her.

This room had become a very comfortable place for Cassandra. It had become a place of thought and of calmness, and it had become a place that she didn't fear as much as she once had. All of the memories of Tigger as a kitten the size of her hand were in this Cage.

He'd gotten so much bigger. She remembered the first time she had tried to feed him and how he'd hissed at her when she tried to pet him while he ate. There were a lot of good memories in this room, and even though it had been a cage, it had certainly not been the worst cage she'd ever experienced.

There would be many good memories of this room.

But it was time to go. It was time to say goodbye to this tiny world and go back to the outside world.

Cassandra took a bite of the cupcake.

Chapter 53

Monster,

  I know that it is insane, but I believe that I will miss you and this Cage. Life is simple here, and the more I've come to know you, the more I think that I could enjoy spending time with you.

  But a cage is a cage, and I cannot live in one ever again. You have shown me kindness as well, and I will forever be grateful that you did not treat me like the monster that I named you.

  I hope that you find your burgeoning soul to be all that you had hoped for. Remember that you must water all things that grow, and souls need emotion to grow. Try to find a way to experience emotions, dear Monster. Preferably without putting anyone in a cage. It's a rude practice, and I do not condone it.

  I was sad to see that you did not give me a question. I've spent too many days and nights thinking on your questions to be able to leave this Cage without one to ponder. Maybe you could give me one when you return me to the civilized world. I think I'd like that. A question to remember you by.

  I will enjoy my celebratory cupcake. I'm glad you didn't use the red icing or else I wouldn't have been able to stomach it, and I'd have been forced to stay here with you.

  I wish you well, Monster. I will not lie to the police when they question me, but I have no information to give them, nor will I think too hard on the questions they give me. You should not be worried.

I have a question for you, a question for the road. "What would you do if I stayed?"

Cassandra Matheson

Chapter 54

50 Days Since the Cage, Age 31

A king-sized bed with slate gray sheets. She knew this bed.

She was home.

She stretched out and heard the insistent meowing. She rolled over and looked down at the kitten in its cage on her floor. Tigger was home with her. And he was pissed. Who knew how long she'd been asleep?

She stretched out. She was wearing a dress she'd never seen before. Silver and black. Sparkling with rhinestones that looked like stars on a midnight sky.

She curled up with her pillow and felt something hard under her hand. She pulled it out. It was a rectangular sign that said, "Welcome Home." and underneath the words were a mirror that had cracks running all through it.

The copper had tarnished into a mixture of blues and greens on top of the copper that made it almost look like it was meant to be at a beach house. She held the sign up and looked in the mirror, and she could see herself in it, barely. It was scratched and looked like someone had drug it behind a car. But you could still see yourself in it.

Under the sign was a letter. The last letter she'd ever get from Monster. She hesitated to read it. She had no idea what to expect from the letter. She'd hoped that she would gain her freedom, but now that she had it, she hoped that Monster was going to be okay.

Something had happened between them when he'd made love to her. It had been different than she'd expected. She'd thought that she would give the experience to him. She'd had sex with plenty of men when she hadn't been interested. It was something that you did as a woman.

It hadn't ended that way though. Instead, she had lost herself in the sensations and in whatever else had been there between the two of them. It had been a more intense sexual experience than she had ever felt, and it had felt good.

She was not a sexual person. She didn't turn men down when she was dating them, but she didn't typically enjoy it.

She had enjoyed this. More than she'd ever expected from sex with anyone much less a man she still had never seen.

Cassandra took a deep breath as she tore open the envelope with a satisfying ripping sound. In all of the time that Monster and she had sent letters back and forth to each other, this was the first and only letter that she was able to actually open which seemed strange.

She flipped the papers open and began to read.

Chapter 55

Cassandra,

You asked what I would do if you had decided to stay, and the answer is simple. I would open the door and leave the light on. I have no desire to keep you captive any longer, but until you decide to stay with me of your own free will, I cannot give you that freedom. I would not want to expect you to lie for my protection.

Now, you have absolutely no way to tell anyone who abducted you or where you were. I have saved you from a choice once again, but it is necessary for both of us to stay protected.

Cassandra, I will miss you more than anything in the world. I cannot simply leave you. Not yet. No, I will not interfere in your life any more than I did before the incident with Craig. You do not have to worry about being abducted again. I would die before I forced you to do anything else.

I simply will watch you. I don't know what else to do. You were more than an obsession, Cassandra. You were more than a love. You were my life. And I do not know what to do without you. So I will watch you as I have watched you for the last thirteen years. Ever since you left your foster parents' house, I have watched you.

Never did I expect to abduct you. But I do not regret it. I will never regret taking you and keeping you. You may hate me because of it, and I would not blame you. I too have been forced into cages.

You are a beautiful, intelligent, funny, and more than anything else, caring woman. You should never be forced to be with people who do not recognize this for what it is.

If you ever decide that you would prefer a life with me, all you need to do is hang the sign I have given you on your door. I will see it, and I will bring you to me.

I love you Cassandra. I think I always have. And I certainly always will. You have been a light in my darkness, and though we both now know how to walk through the darkness, I think that maybe the light is more enjoyable.

I hope to speak and maybe make love to you again, but if you decide against it, remember that at least one person understands you, and one person will never let you down.

You asked for a question for the road, and I'll ask you the same one that I asked you when you first woke up in the Cage. "How do you still care so much about everyone?" I think that there's more to it than what you've told me.

William

Chapter 56

55 Days Since the Cage, Age 31

Cassandra walked into the kitchen where a very nervous woman sat. She still had sores healing on her cheeks from the meth. They *were* healing though. Two children ran around the house chasing each other with toy guns. They wore what looked to be clean clothes and no shoes.

She glanced at the sink and saw a handful of dishes waiting to be washed. Stacy Williams was trying. Anyone could see the difference.

The first time Cassandra had walked into her home, a small three-bedroom house that she'd inherited from her mother, the home had smelled like something had died in it. Cigarette butts had littered the floors, and rotten food had been spilling out of the trashcan.

Most of the walls had little holes in them where someone had gotten angry and hit them. That was the life of a meth head.

When Cassandra had met Stacy, she'd scratched at her arms continuously, and her face had been a mess of sores. She had looked like she hadn't showered or brushed her hair in weeks. The two little boys had been running around naked throwing trash at each other.

The house was not perfectly clean. Cassandra didn't expect it to be. The floors could use a good sweeping. There were bits of food on the stove, but it was crumbs from breakfast or dinner last night. This was not a well cleaned house, but it was not a dangerous house.

She sat down at the table with Stacy. "Good morning, Stacy. How are you doing?"

Stacy looked pointedly at the boys who were still screaming and running around the house chasing each other. "Some days are a struggle. Joey and Sam still act like I'm on dope," she said as she sipped a cup of coffee.

"Do you want some?" she asked indicating her coffee cup. "No thank you," Cassandra said as she watched Stacy. Stacy still shook some. It was hard to deal with two young boys who screamed when you were struggling to get clean. She knew that.

"They're going to be difficult. You're learning to be a mom, Stacy. They've never really had that before. Take it slow. That's all you can do."

"Yeah." She sighed. "That's all I can do." Silence hung in the air before it was broken by the two boys yelling.

"How are you holding up?" Stacy asked her. "I missed you. You get it all better than that other woman that came by while you were gone."

She paused for a moment before continuing, "If you need to talk to someone, you can talk to me. I've been with some real fucked up guys, but I've never been kept in a room for months." She took another sip of her coffee while she waited for Cassandra to tell her all about it. It was odd how everyone wanted to talk to her about her captivity.

Cassandra passed it off as their curiosity and not for callousness. She wasn't as filled with trauma as so many of them expected. Then again, her captor had not been cruel, unlike most of the captors in the news and stories.

Monster, no it was William. That's how he had signed his last letter. But she'd never called him William. Her mind couldn't wrap itself around that name. No, she decided, he would stay Monster in her mind. At least until she called him William to his face.

That's when she realized that she had already begun thinking about talking to him again.

She blinked, trying to get away from her thoughts long enough to focus on the woman sitting at the table with her.

"It wasn't as bad as people think. He was kind. At least as kind as I could possibly expect a man to be when he had me captive."

"Girl, he wasn't kind. That's the crazy talking. No one abducts someone and then is kind. That's not the way that men's minds work. He had you, and he could do whatever he wanted to you. A man doesn't get that power over a woman and then give it up. It's just not how their minds work."

Cassandra looked at the woman. Looked at her scar and sore covered face. She'd known plenty of men who would take advantage of a woman, plenty of men who had hurt women. She hadn't known Monster, though. That was the difference, wasn't it?

She knew actual monsters, not her Monster.

"He wasn't as bad as he could have been, but I'm here about you today Stacy. Has Aaron tried to come back to see you or the kids?"

"No, we're done. I'm not going to put my kids through his bullshit, excuse my French. If he comes back to my house, I'll call the cops. I'm not going to lose my kids over him. Specially now that I'm clean."

"Good." Cassandra replied, nodding her head. "The house is looking a lot better. You're doing well."

Stacy's haggard look brightened a little at the compliment. "I'm trying. I really am. It's hard though. I had no idea how hard it would be. I've been a mother for eight years, but I'm just now learning how to be a mom, though. It makes me want to run back to the dope, but then I look at those boys, and I remember that I'll lose 'em if I start back up. That's the only thing keeping me clean, you know?"

Cassandra nodded again. "Everyone that gets away from drugs has something to anchor them, Stacy. For you, it may be the boys. For others, it's their family. For others, it's some event. Everyone needs that anchor. At least at first. Eventually, you'll learn to live without it, but for now, just keep them in your thoughts."

"That's what I'm doing. It's the only thing I can do. That, and just keep trying to fix this damned house. Who knew how tore up it really was? I had to climb up on the roof last week and patch it myself. Couldn't afford to hire someone, and it keeps leaking in the bathroom. How'd I go four years without knowing the roof leaked?" She looked at Cassandra as though she expected a response.

"Well Stacy, I think a lot of that had to do with the fact that the house was disgusting for those four years."

Stacy nodded. "Yeah. It's like someone gave me a pair of glasses for the first time and I can see the world clearly. Like someone wiped away all the fog. No one could have explained it to me back then. I sure am glad I got clean."

"Me too, Stacy. Me too." Cassandra stood up. "Well, it seems like things are going well enough with you. Keep up the hard work, and if you need anything, don't hesitate to call me." She patted Stacy's shoulder. "You're doing it. You're going to be fine, and those boys are going to grow up with a real mom."

Stacy looked up at Cassandra with hopeful eyes. "I'm trying."

Cassandra nodded and said, "That's all you can do."

Chapter 57

Tigger raced around the covers of the king-sized bed before leaping to the floor and tackling the little ball that was powered by a small motor. He rolled around with it for a second before kicking it off him and jumping back on the bed.

His ears laid back on his head as he rushed off the bed again to pounce on the ball as it continued to roll. He'd gotten so big. She looked at him as he kicked the ball across the room again and made it back to the top of the bed in no time flat.

Cassandra reached out and grabbed him under his front legs, disregarding the obvious danger to her hands. He stopped trying to race off and looked at her. The motor inside the ball kept spinning, and the little ball of fluff continued to roll around the room.

Tigger looked at it as it moved, but then turned back to Cassandra, completely calm. He hadn't always been like this, so docile while being held. And no one had trained him to calm down. He'd just figured out that clawing Cassandra while she held him was hurting her, and he stopped doing it.

He nuzzled her cheek as she held him to her chest. It was hard to be back in the real world. Monster had been right. The police had questioned her numerous times over the course of that first week. They'd had no leads and had given up the search for her already when she arrived home.

Now that she was home, they were back on the hunt for the man who'd kidnapped her. They wouldn't find him. Just like they hadn't found him when he'd killed Craig. Somehow, the memory of that had no effect on her anymore. It was like she was looking at memories of someone else in her mind.

The emotions that she'd once had for the man who had killed Craig, namely anger and rage, were no longer there. She understood that he hadn't meant to hurt her, and though she still believed that Monster had been in the wrong, the thought behind the action had been for her benefit.

Tigger purred as she held him. How did he do that? Go from insane murder kitten to cuddly floof ball in less than a minute? She laid back on the bed and curled up to the kitten who was now nearly as long as her arm and weighed several pounds.

"Sometimes, the world just doesn't make very much sense, does it?" Everyone she talked to had told her to go home and rest. She'd tried to tell them that she wasn't traumatized, wasn't afraid, and wasn't tired. They'd tried to tell her that she was wrong, that she needed the rest, that she'd had such a hard time.

They didn't believe her. She had told them exactly what she'd needed, to get back to work, and they'd ignored her. Luckily, she worked on her own schedule, so she just did it anyways.

It had been almost two weeks since she'd gotten home, and it still didn't feel like home yet. Tigger had warmed up to it, and he'd enjoyed all of the new toys she'd bought him. He still went back to his cage regularly though. It was like he could enjoy his freedom, but when it was time to rest, he wanted the safety of the cage.

Cassandra could relate to him. She felt so exposed here. If she'd told people that, they would have assumed she meant that she was afraid Monster would come for her, but he was the last person she was worried about. In fact, the idea that he watched her was the greatest comfort that she had.

Was this fear of being exposed something she'd lived with her entire life? Had her captivity truly been the first time she'd ever felt safe?

She'd grown up with the fear of monsters hiding behind every corner. She'd lived with the need to hide herself and her voice at all times. She'd grown up and moved away, but there had been no greater safety away from her foster parents. Not truly. The people of the world were still cruel and terrible creatures.

She'd bought a home and locked her doors, but she knew just how easy it was to break into a house. There was very little safety in her home. She smiled at Tigger. She had one protector at least. She remembered the time that he'd attacked Monster even when he'd been a tiny little thing.

He showed her his teeth in his impression of a smile which seemed absolutely terrifying. And adorable.

There had been only one time that she had felt safe. The Cage was nothingness, was darkness, but for the first time in her life, a Monster guarded her instead of hunted her.

Would she be able to stay with him? Would she be able to leave the rest of the world behind? He would never fit in the normal world. Not the way that he would have to for her to continue living her life.

Cassandra put Tigger down on the bed, and he immediately went from docile lap cat to murderous creature. Racing away from her, he leapt off the bed and hit the ball with full force. He bit and scratched at it before kicking it away from him again and racing up the side of her bed.

Maybe he really was a Monster, just like Tigger. Tigger would do his absolute best to kill anything and anyone he felt was a threat or food. Mouse or man, Tigger wouldn't care.

Maybe she just felt more at home with monsters. Maybe they made her feel safe.

Chapter 58

67 Days Since the Cage, Age 31

Officer Joe Walsh laughed deeply as he sat across from Cassandra inside his office.

"You're insane, Cassie. How are you already working? You were abducted. Things… things happened to you. And, here we are a couple weeks later. You working like nothing happened at all."

"Joe, don't treat me like everyone else does. Those kids need my help. That's what keeps me going. You know how it is." She was serious even though she wore a smile on her face.

"Cassie, someone else can handle your cases for a while." He scratched the thinning hair on top of his head. He'd done that same motion his entire life when he was confused or frustrated with a conversation.

"But can they do them as well as I can?" she said softly. "Do they understand those kids and those homes as well as I do?"

Joe looked away knowingly. He knew her past. He knew a lot of things that most people didn't understand. "You should still take care of yourself so that you can keep taking care of the kids," he said softly, no longer confident in himself.

Joe was a boy when the worst years of her life had happened. He hadn't known what to do. He hadn't known how to help. Neither had Cassandra for that matter. She should have gone to the police. She could have proven it to someone.

But that hadn't been how things were handled while she was growing up. You didn't tell the police, no matter what. You didn't even ask for help from the other kids. You simply survived.

"Joe, just treat me like I'd never been kidnapped, okay? The rest of the world, and all of your coworkers can fuss and worry over me, but not you, okay?"

He nodded to her.

"Did you get me the files I asked for?" Cassandra asked.

He nodded again before leaning on the desk. "Why do you want them? I mean, you didn't even know him back then. Nobody did."

"I knew him better than you think." Cassandra's eyes were piercing as she stared Joe down.

"What are you going to do?" he asked as he scratched the top of his head again. No wonder he was losing his hair.

"Nothing. I just wanted to know that he was okay."

"Oh, okay," he said as he fished out some files from a desk drawer. "I went back the last ten years. There weren't any files before that. It was like he didn't exist."

Cassandra nodded as she took the files and put them into her purse. "Joe, I really am okay. You know that, right?"

He nodded absentmindedly before focusing on her, "Yeah. I just worry about you sometimes. You aren't always the safest person I know."

She grinned at him. "I wouldn't be as good at my job if I was worried about being safe."

He shook his head slowly. "Maybe your safety is more important to me than your performance."

Chapter 59

26 years before the Cage, Age 5

Her hair was long and tied up in a ponytail with a ribbon woven into it. The dress Cassandra wore was bright and new with Easter colors. Pinks and blues and greens and yellows all mixed together.

Miss Faith rode in the trailer with Cassandra while Big Tony drove the lawn mower. He was driving fast, and he didn't slow down for the bumps. Each time they hit a bump, Cassandra would bounce up a few inches before falling back down on the hay bale she was using as a seat. Her tinkling laughter filled the air each time.

Miss Faith was all smiles then. Her hip hurt something fierce, but she wouldn't be talked out of watching Cassandra's first hayride. It wasn't their lawn mower or trailer. Big Tony was using it to move the hay bales from one building to another for work, but when he'd told Miss Faith about it, she had insisted that they go with him.

They'd been riding for almost an hour now, and still Cassandra was laughing at every bump. Miss Faith was glad that she hadn't let the pain stop her from coming with Cassandra and Big Tony. This was a memory she'd remember for a long time. It wasn't often that she could find things that were worth getting out of bed for these days, and almost all of them had something to do with Cassandra.

When they got to the barn for Big Tony to unload the hay, Miss Faith said, "Honey, I think I'm going to have to be done with hayrides for a while." Cassandra looked at her sharply, finally noticing the grimace that Miss Faith couldn't keep from her face.

"Is your hip hurtin' Miss Faith?" she asked as she hopped of the trailer. She raised her hand to steady Miss Faith as she limped off. She stood by to steady the older woman as she hobbled to a chair sitting inside the barn.

"Darlin', my hip is always hurtin'. You know that. But it was worth it. No doubt about that. Pain ain't nothin' to a woman my age. Seein' you enjoy yourself like that was better than any TV I'd be watchin'."

Cassandra watched her like a bird, head cocked to the side in confusion. "You're okay hurtin' to see me have fun?"

Miss Faith laughed softly, and a big smile filled her face as she said, "Of course, Cassandra. Why wouldn't I? You and Big Tony are the only reasons why I'm still stickin' around after all. There ain't much left of my life other than you two."

Cassandra sat down in front of her and began to pick the clover that covered the ground. "What do you mean by that? I don't understand."

"Well, you think about a person, okay? They go through life. Life beats 'em up real good. Bad stuff happens.

They get sad, and they cry. They get over it, right? Most of the time at least?"

She paused for a minute to let the image settle in Cassandra's young mind. "It's like they're a window that life taps with different sized hammers. Some are little taps and some are big hard smacks. Things like my hip bein' hurt is one of them big smacks. Well, eventually, if nobody comes by to take care of that window, if nobody puts the pieces back together, eventually, there ain't no window left, ya hear?"

"But see, sometimes a real sweet, real nice man or woman or child comes by, and they pick up some of them pieces and they put 'em back in place. Now, they'll stick for a while all by themselves, but eventually, life's gonna come by and smack that window real good and shake 'em all loose."

Cassandra looked up at Miss Faith. "Well, how come the nice man don't glue 'em together like you did with that cup I broke?"

"Well darlin', that's not so easy. Not everybody has the patience. Not everybody is willing to hold it still and let it set, and not everybody's got the glue. See, that glue is love, sweetheart. It's why people get married and have babies."

"Cause that man and woman, they come into it all broken up like everybody else. Then they start puttin' each other's pieces together, and they start gluin' 'em together. All those whacks that life's given 'em, well, they don't matter so much anymore."

"When you and Big Tony is around and happy, my ol' hip don't matter so much. You keep me from fallin' apart, little miss. And Big Tony, he keeps on gluin' me back together even when life whacks me real good."

"How do I keep you from fallin' apart?" Cassandra asked softly.

"Just by bein' here. Just by lovin' me and huggin' me and bein' the sweetest little miss I've ever met." Miss Faith felt the tears begin to fall softly down her cheek.

Cassandra stood up and gave her a big hug, trying not to bump her hurt hip.

"Now," she said as she sniffled, "you'd better go get back on that trailer and do some more ridin' around so that no more of my pieces fall apart, ya hear?" Cassandra nodded and gave Miss Faith a kiss on the cheek.

"I love you, Miss Faith. I think that you and Big Tony glued me together after my ma and pa died."

"Maybe we did, and maybe we didn't, little miss. Either way, if ya don't go get on that trailer, I'm gonna have ta get Big Tony after ya."

Cassandra gave her a big smile and ran off towards the trailer.

Chapter 60

Cassandra drove up the mountain slowly, savoring the warm afternoon air. The pine trees were thick here. She drove with the windows down, taking in the scents and sounds of the forest.

The road was a twisting set of switchbacks, each of which gave a better view of the overlooking forest and mountains. It would be a beautiful view from the top. Cassandra tried to stay focused on the road though. Between the view and the thoughts racing through her mind, it was difficult to stay focused on anything.

She'd made the decision yesterday to drive to the house. She hadn't been sure until she had the file, but once she saw what was in it… Well, it all made sense now. All of it.

When she arrived at the building at the end of the long driveway, she was impressed. He'd done well for himself. Blocky stone walls rose from the mountain, like castle walls. Parapets rose on the sides, and she almost expected to see men with guns resting atop them.

A fortress set into the mountain itself waited for her, and she had to take several breaths before she could convince herself to leave her car. Ahead of her, a set of massive wooden double doors were closed against the world. On either side of them were bronze sconces set into the stone walls.

She finally managed to step out onto the gravel. One step in front of the other, she walked to the front door. She didn't knock. She swiftly hung the sign that Monster had given her around the sconce on the right of the door. Before she left, though, she pulled a letter from her pocket.

She slipped it into the mail drop and turned around. She would soon find out if she'd been correct.

Chapter 61

He stared at the walls. That's all he could do. Darkness, walls, and a bed. There was the bucket too. Once upon a time, he'd used a toilet, but it had been years. He only had the bucket now.

He stared at the wood grains that he'd traced with his eyes for years. The same wood grains. He could have drawn the room with his eyes closed. Every inch of it was committed to memory. Not because he had wanted to, but because there was absolutely nothing else to do.

Years. He'd been in this room for ten years. He only had two more. That's what the notes said at least. She'd found out for him. He'd never known how long he'd been in the room before her.

That had been kind of her. He didn't know why she was being kind to him. No one else was. He wasn't entirely sure that anyone else even knew he was there. He knew that they were. He could hear them. Always.

He heard them talking about their days. They whispered, but he heard them anyways. He heard them cleaning and working. He heard them getting punished. That was happening more now. Something had changed.

He didn't understand what had changed. He didn't understand a lot of things about the other children. They weren't like him though. He was crazy. He heard them talk about him like that sometimes. Especially when they saw her do something nice for him.

He opened his eyes when he heard the slip of paper slide under the door. He smiled. It was the only time he smiled. His one letter a day from the girl.

He stood up silently and retrieved the letter. There was no light in the room except from the crack under the door, so he laid down on his back and read by the light.

Chapter 62

Billy,

It was a good day today. The teacher liked the report I gave her. I got an A. She said that I needed to be more confident. She said that I tended to be too shy. I thought about you when she said that. I wonder what she'd say about you.

Would you like to leave the room, or would it all be too much? You've been in there so long that I'd think that it would hard to be around people now. Did you like to be around people before they put you in there? I like people, I think. At least enough to not want to live under the stairs.

That would be hard for me. How do you do it? What do you do down there? Do you ever just get mad and hit things? That's what I'd do probably. I'd hit things until I broke out or until they took me out for making such a racket. Or until I died.

I think I'd rather be dead than be stuck down there. I hope you don't die though. I think I'd miss you a lot. You've only got two years left, Billy. Remember that. You're so close.

Susan says that she's only got three more years until she leaves forever. Paul said he wasn't ever coming back, but then he came back and hit Mr. George. I don't think he'll come back now though. Will you come back when they can't put you under the stairs?

Will you come back and see me? I'd like to see you. I'd like to get to know you. Maybe I could teach you some games. I'm patient. You can ask Joe. He's not very good at them, but I helped him get better at lots of them.

Just two more years, Billy. That's all. Then you can come out. Then you can come play with us.

I hope you have a good day tomorrow. I'll look for your letter before Miss Franny wakes up. Remember, just put the tip out or she'll see it.

Cassie Matheson

Chapter 63

13 years before the Cage, Age 18

The headstones were simple but beautiful. Gray granite that had been etched with yellow lettering. There were no flowers on their graves. No one had visited them. They hadn't had anyone.

Faith Walker. 1947-1999. Loving Wife.

Tony Walker. 1945-1998. Loving Husband.

Miss Faith had died when she was ten. Big Tony had died when she was nine. Cassandra had the newspaper clippings of their obituaries. Tony had battled cancer for five years until it finally won. That was why he'd had to quit his job.

Faith had known that she would never adopt her. She had known that Tony and she would never come save her. They'd done what they could to give her hope.

Cassandra shook her head as she looked at the graves. They'd had no one. No children and no family. She'd been the last good thing that they'd experienced. They'd been the last good thing that she'd experienced as well.

That's why she'd immediately gone in search of Faith and Tony when she'd aged out of her foster home. She'd needed to find them. They'd been the last good things that she could remember about the world. Everything else had become... wrong.

Miss Faith and Big Tony were dead though. Long dead. Cassandra knew she should be crying, but she couldn't. She should be mourning the loss of her last good memories, should be mourning the loss of the last good people she knew.

But she couldn't.

There were no more tears. Not for the good or the bad. Not for anyone else. She let the newspaper clippings go, and they fluttered on the wind, never to be seen by her again.

Through it all. Through the abuse, through the pain, through the misery, she'd always held onto that bit of hope that when she aged out, she would get to see Faith and Tony again. She had dreamed of the moment an uncountable number of times. She'd imagined the tears of joy that they'd all shed.

She'd held onto that hope. Those two would be able to fix her. They'd be able to show her how to be happy again. They'd done it once before when she'd started to crack as a child. They'd put those pieces back together and made her whole again.

But now they were gone. There was no one left. No family. No friends. No one.

And the pieces she'd been desperately trying to hold together fell apart. There would be no glue to hold them together.

Chapter 64

Monster,

If you have received this, then I expect to see you again soon. You left me with a question, and for the first time, I have an answer. You asked how I still care so much. I will finally, after all of these years, reveal to someone else the truth on this matter.

I don't. I don't care about the children any more than you care about your mother and father. I know that I should. I know that Joe and Susan and Paul would. I take care of people because that's what you're supposed to do.

I learned a long time ago how to fit in. That's really all the difference between the two of us is. I have friends because I'm supposed to. I have boyfriends because I'm supposed to. I became a social worker because I have to have a job, and I knew I would be good at it. Especially since I don't care.

I told you when we first began talking about love that I loved only four people. That was the truth. I have never felt the emotion toward another person again. Until now. Now, I'm not sure that it's the truth. Not when I think about you.

I named you Monster, and I will continue to call you Monster for the irony. You are the first person I have known since I met Miss Franny and Mr. George that was not a monster.

You have been with me since I left them. You were the one who made sure that nothing else bad ever happened to me. I know. I had your background checked, and you've been within easy driving distance from me my entire adult life.

How many times did you protect me? How many times did you keep the monsters in the dark from hurting me? How many times when I was blackout drunk in college did you save me?

I wish that you could have been there when I broke, when I became nothing. Maybe it wouldn't have happened. But Monster, I think that maybe you're the only one who could help put me back together.

Making love to you was the first time that I have felt anything since I was broken.

Will you help me to feel, Monster? Will you help me to love? Will you help me to care?

I do not know if I love you. What I am sure of is that if there is a key to the Cage of nothingness inside of me, it lies in your hands. Will you try to find it with me?

I have many questions, but the one question I will ask is, "Will you take me back even if I'm more broken than you?"

Cassie Matheson

Chapter 65

69 Days Since the Cage, Age 31

Cassandra's eyes fluttered open. Her head rested on a pillow. A pillow on a twin bed with white sheets. She sat up straight and realized that she was still dressed. A little dismayed at not being naked, she looked around.

She was in the Cage again, and she heard the frustrated scratching and meowing of Tigger next to the bed.

The walls hadn't been fixed. The pile of gifts was still sitting in the corner where she'd left it. Everything was exactly how she'd left it. With two exceptions.

One, the door with no peep hole was open, inviting her to walk through it.

Two, a man sat in the chair at her desk.

"Good morning, Cassandra. I'm glad that you're awake. We have a very busy day planned."

Cassandra rubbed the sleep out of her eyes and yawned as she stepped out of the bed.

"Monster?" she said softly as she looked at the man in the chair. Blond hair, cut short and styled as though he were getting ready for a magazine photo shoot. A neatly trimmed thin beard that framed his face. A scar that cut across his left eyebrow, breaking the otherwise perfect symmetry of his face.

And emerald eyes. Eyes that had watched her for more than a decade. Eyes that knew every inch of her body. Eyes that had seen her at her best and her worst.

"Yes, Cassandra. Or William. Or Billy. You can call me what you wish. I will call you Cassandra because it carries none of the taint of that house," he said. His voice didn't sound the same in the light of day. It had less gravel to it, less intensity.

Or was that because she wasn't used to the silence anymore?

"Monster in private, and William in public," she said as she walked up to him. "I see that you were willing to take me back. I'm glad."

"Me too," he said. He stood up and put his hand around her waist. "Though, after today, I think that you may need to go back to your previous attire. I found it very pleasing."

"Whatever you feel is right. You've trusted me for a long time, Monster. I think that maybe it's time for me to trust you a little more."

He leaned down and pressed his lips against hers, not wasting any time. He pulled back before he got lost in her. "We will have plenty of time for that soon enough. I have a present for you. A gift for the woman that I love."

Confusion filled her face as she let him pull back. "What kind of gift?"

"The only kind that matters. The kind that will let you finally heal." He smiled at her, showing a bit of teeth. "I have a few things that you get to break."

Chapter 66

She opened her eyes. Her entire body hurt, and she couldn't quite figure out why. She tried to stretch, but her arms were stuck. She looked around and realized that she was strapped to something. Fog seemed to cloud everything in her mind.

She couldn't remember how she'd gotten here. She'd been eating dinner with her husband, and then… that's all. Nothing else. She didn't remember going to bed, didn't remember washing her dishes. For all she knew, the cake that had been in the oven was still there.

She shook her head and looked around. George was there. His body was strapped to a table, just as she was. His arms and legs were held by ropes to the wood that he lay on. He was naked.

She looked down at herself and realized that she'd been stripped of her clothes as well. She began to shake. What was happening? Where was she?

She looked at the table that lay between them. On it lay knifes and all manner of things that could only be used for torturing someone.

"George!" she hissed in a whisper. He began to wake, and she hissed his name again, this time louder.

"What's going on, Franny?" he said with his eyes still closed. "George! Wake up! We were drugged!"

He struggled to open his eyes and look around. Franny watched him realize what was happening and then realize that the both of them were naked. It was the exact same sequence of events that Franny had experienced only moments before.

"Where are we Franny?" he whispered, his eyes wide with fear.

"I don't know! Do you remember anything?" she asked. Her eyes kept going back to the door, back to where whatever monster had captured her would come from.

"No. Nothing after dinner. Why would someone take us?"

"I don't know." They were quiet for a few moments, and then the door opened, and a woman walked into the room.

"Good evening, Miss Franny and Mr. George." They both turned to look at the woman walking towards them.

Brown hair, mousy, soft tan skin, petite. "Let us go!" Franny said in a panic as she pulled on her restraints.

"No Franny, I don't think that I'll be letting you go. You didn't let me go, and you didn't let Billy go either." Cassandra walked in front of her foster parents, an evil smile on her lips.

"Do you remember me?" she asked. George nodded to her slowly, and Franny didn't make a sound, but her eyes grew wide. She knew her. She knew what this was about now.

"I thought you would remember. We spent so many hours together," she said, her voice filled with a false nostalgia. Cassandra walked towards the table and picked up a small knife. Its handle was black, but the blade was a smooth silvery steel.

"Do you know why you're here, Franny?" she asked as she carried the knife to her foster mother. She held the knife at her waist as she stood a foot away from the older woman.

"Because... because of what George did to you?" she said with furtive glances at her husband. Cassandra brought the knife to Franny's neck, and she let the blade trace a wrinkle, not putting any pressure on her thin skin.

"No, Miss Franny," she said with a smile. "You can't blame someone else this time. See, I'm not a child anymore. I'm not powerless, and I'm not being forced to accept anything."

"You're not here because I'm angry anymore." She paused and moved the knife down Franny's chest, moving toward her breast. "You're here for your punishment. You were always so fond of punishments. I'm here as your judge, jury, and executioner, and there is no lie that you can tell me to get out of it."

Footsteps sounded as another person entered the room. Blonde hair and emerald eyes. A scar across his left eyebrow and a smile that refused to go away. "And I will stand as witness," Monster said.

George had been afraid before, but now he shook in his restraints. He pulled against them, and his fat belly shook with effort as he tried to get away. "Oh, so you remember me, Mr. George. The crazy one."

"Are you going to kill us?" Franny said softly as tears fell down her cheeks.

"Eventually," Cassandra said as she pressed the knife softly against the skin of the woman's breast and slowly dragged it downward. A faint line of red rose to the surface, and Franny pulled hard against the bindings as she shrieked.

"You can't do this! You have to let us go!" she cried, and George looked at her dumbly. He didn't have any answers for her this time.

"Yes, we can, and yes, we will. But don't be scared, Miss Franny. You aren't going to die yet. You held Billy captive for twelve years under the stairs, and you raped me for two years. I'm sure that we'll be able to keep you alive for at least a year or two. It wouldn't be justice otherwise."

She smiled at Monster. "This was the best present you could have given me."

"A gift of blood and pain and vengeance," he said softly as he walked up behind her.

"Yes, dearest Monster, they're perfect."

He wrapped his arms around her waist, and she could feel his strength. She felt safe in those arms. He had caught the monsters and he had brought them to her.

He had known her better than anyone else. He had kept her safe when no one else had been able to. She felt pieces begin to shift inside of her. He bent his head down to her neck and kissed her slowly.

She looked at her captives who stared at her in fear. The same fear that she'd felt so many times as a child. And she smiled. For the first time in her life since she'd been taken from Miss Faith and Big Tony, she felt like someone might be able to put her pieces back together.

"I hope you enjoy breaking them, my love," Monster said gently in Cassandra's ear.

"I will." Cassandra wasn't sure how she felt. But something was changing, and she felt happy for the first time since she was five. But it was more than that, more than happy. She felt like her Monster might be strong enough, patient enough, and caring enough to be the glue for the broken pieces inside of her.

"Thank you for being my Monster," she said softly.

"I couldn't be anything else."

"And I love you for it," she said.